TO TAME A ROGUE

KELLY JAMESON

Kelly Jameson is the author of DEAD ON, which Kat Martin, NYT best-selling author, calls "Brilliant." It's the story of a medical examiner being chased through time by the same killer.

Best-selling crime noir author Ken Bruen calls Kelly Jameson's psychological suspense SHARDS OF SUMMER, "The Great Gatsby for the beach generation."

WHAT REMAINED OF KATRINA: A NOVEL OF NEW ORLEANS, Kelly Jameson's novella, was a Leapfrog Press Honorable Mention in fiction. "What Remained of Katrina becomes a powerful story of the city's underclass, the one seldom reported by the media, the one seldom visited by tourists. This is Jameson's third novel, and may be the best one yet." Walter Brasch, Journalist/Author

1

Louisiana, 1816

"This grubby urchin' is my *betrothed*?" Nicholas Branton was

incredulous. His words were blunt, his look insulting.

Good, Camille thought, watching the pair briefly in amusement

before dropping her eyes to the floor. It was working. She had

dressed in the plainest, baggiest clothes, had hidden her long, honey-

colored hair beneath a soiled and rumpled cap, and had kept her

green eyes downcast while shifting on her feet.

For all intents and purposes, she was what she appeared to be—

a street wench, an unkempt nobody. It was exactly the impression

she wanted to give Nicholas Branton.

Surely he would take one look at her and the arrangement would

fall through. What was her uncle thinking anyway, arranging for her to marry some bootlicker? Camille fumed; despite her lack of wealth or prospects, her whole being rebelled against the idea! And what kind of man would agree to a marriage with a woman he had never even met, let alone a woman of her...ilk...as society called it?

There was still time. As far as she knew, no date had been set for the wedding, which wouldn't take place at all if Camille could help it. This was going to be too easy. Her mood lightened, her confidence grew.

"Genevieve, have you lost your mind?"

Genevieve stood in her brother's impressive shadow, speechless for once.

"This can't possibly be Penley's niece." He looked directly at Camille. "Who put you up to this?"

Camille spoke to the floor, anger building along with her confidence. "Mister, maybe you should send me on my way now....I can ride a horse and I don't need no escort. I could be back afore night fall, and we'll just forget about this whole foolish idee."

It was the first time Camille had spoken, other than a few grunts and groans and nods of her head, since the Branton coach with its

2

black and gold piping and heavy leather doors had come to collect

her that afternoon. Fortunately, Camille's uncle had been so

engrossed at the gaming tables that he hadn't noticed her slipping

out of the tavern. Not that he would have recognized her with her

cap pulled low over her face. He never paid much attention anyway.

She'd borrowed the tattered cap and the shabby breeches from a

lad who worked the kitchens. The homespun blouse she wore was

her own, and usually reserved for kitchen drudgery—the threads of

the garment held together now only by some divine force. Like the

other serving girls, she had to wear more revealing clothing of a

slightly higher quality when she waited on customers. Her uncle had

spared coin for that; pretty serving girls meant more customers.

Beyond that, she'd never owned anything lavish or fancy.

Nicholas had been too busy to meet her himself, so Genevieve

met her just outside the tavern—something Camille was sure would

add to the sordid impression she sought to create.

To her credit, and to Camille's dismay, Genevieve hadn't

looked down on her in any way. In fact, Genevieve had seemed

content to chatter away during most of the ride, filling the awkward silence as if they'd known each other a lifetime and not just a few moments.

Camille's uncle had no idea that she'd arranged this meeting with Nicholas Branton. She hadn't wasted much time planning it after her uncle had informed her of her impending betrothal to the man. Her uncle had been her 'guardian' since her parents' deaths; he expected total obedience from her. He'd told her, on more than one occasion, that her wishes would not sway him from his plans in the least, and that she should be grateful for the match.

She hoped to be back after dusk to work her shift at the tavern with none the wiser, her goal accomplished. If she wasn't back there would be hell to pay from Mother Stephens.

"Girl, are you Camille Hardison? Look at me."

Camille slowly lifted her head and found herself staring into the most compelling tawny eyes; they were the color of whiskey, deep and expressive, and tinged with gold flecks. The man was tall, with hair as dark and black as a cold winter's night—a marked contrast to his eyes. His masculine lips quickly jogged into a frown. Or perhaps it was merely distaste. Indeed, though his features were stern, they

4

looked as if they were hewn from stone, his jaw dusted by a shadow of dark whiskers.

Camille felt a fluttering in her stomach—a new uncertainty about what she was doing. Her betrothed was standing, his palms resting on the top of a massive mahogany desk littered with papers, and he was still a full head taller than she was. He continued to stare at her, slight smudges of fatigue beneath his eyes.

"She *is* Penley's niece," Genevieve remarked. "I met her myself outside his tavern."

Camille inched her chin up a notch, craning her neck to look into his eyes. "I'm Camille Hardison, sure enuf, not that it's yer business to judge me mister."

A crooked smile appeared on his face. He dismissed her impatiently with his eyes and addressed his sister.

"Good, she's dirty *and* uppity. Take her upstairs Genny, let her have a good scrubbing, and for God's sake, lend her something to wear. I don't want to see her in those rags again.

"I'll expect the urchin' to be cleaned up for dinner," he grumbled, giving his attention back to the papers on his desk. "I'll

5

verify her birth records for sure," he said, more to himself than to anyone in the room.

Camille couldn't resist speaking her mind, though with each word she spoke, the chances grew greater that she would unknowingly reveal herself. Judging by the look of his masculine study, the volumes of worn leather books on the polished shelves, the papers spread before him, Nicholas Branton was not a stupid man. How long would he be fooled? "Don't go gettin' yourself too attached to me, mister."

Nicholas looked up and arched a winged, dark brow.

"That's not a distinct possibility."

"She'll be cleaned up, Nick," Genevieve interjected quickly. "Follow me, Camille. I'll see you to one of the guestrooms. I'll send Lucy up with some hot water to help you with your bath. I imagine you'll want to get...changed...for dinner? I can loan you something to wear."

"Don't mean to be rude to you, miss, but I'll just be on my way. I'm not changin' out o' these clothes, and I don't see no reason to stay for dinner." She stuck her small chin in the air—it was becoming a habit around this man. "I don't stomach the thought of eatin' with *him* no-how. He hasn't heard a word I said."

Camille moved toward the door. She stopped for a moment, nervously wringing her small hands.

"Thank you for your...hospi...hospitality, miss, and I'm truly sorry ya wasted your time. I'll be happy to tell my uncle the uh...betrothal...is off. I'll just see myself out."

She whisked herself through the door.

"Bloody hell," Genevieve sighed.

Nick cocked an eyebrow. Genevieve's cheeks colored. "What! You say it all the time! Where do you think I learned it?"

He closed one of his ledgers and walked around the desk. "I'm not a lady, dear Sis, so I'm more easily forgiven my vices. You'd best remember that if you're ever to catch a husband." He playfully ruffled Genevieve's hair then stroked his chin.

"Damn me, but that was no lady either." He frowned. "This does complicate matters. Let me go after her."

"What are you doing to do?" she asked. "And by the way, I don't intend to *catch* a husband. You catch colds, dear brother, not husbands."

"I haven't the slightest idea," he replied, heading toward the doorway Camille had just slipped through. "But we're wasting time. One way or another, she's staying. And one way or another, she's going to marry me. I signed a bloody contract, after all, now didn't I?"

"What if I could turn her into a lady?" Genevieve asked.

"Then I'd say you were a damned miracle worker." Nicholas paused between the door and the hallway.

"Don't get any grand ideas," he grumbled. "I'll fulfill my obligations, but it will be a marriage in name only. Thank God the contract doesn't state that I have to love and cherish her. The thought of tolerating that street urchin' for the rest of my life is...."

"Just go get her already! I am quite familiar with your views on marriage, and I don't agree in the least. Just because you had one bad experience...." Genevieve said reproachfully, but her brother's tall form was already out the door.

8

2

Camille skittered down the wide hallways and out onto the massive, pillared front porch. She soon found herself standing in front of the stately mansion, late afternoon sunshine filtering through jade and ivory magnolia leaves that made a canopy above the curving entrance lane. Ancient, twisted limbs arched high above her, mantled in a thick sheen of gold and green from trailing Spanish moss. She was reminded of the gold storm in Nicholas' eyes.

She leaned against one of the columns, which was still warm from the afternoon sun. She hadn't the slightest idea what to do. She hadn't planned how she would get back to the tavern after her little charade. But as the sun sank lower on the horizon, she felt her hopes rising.

She was certain she'd accomplished her goal. She and Nicholas were so different. He was almost everything she'd expected him to be; arrogant, disrespectful, a blue-blood used to getting his way. *All man.*

She did work in a tavern, but she wasn't a lady of pleasure. It had been easy to fool him into thinking she was a wayward tramp, easy to gauge his reactions. He was cultured and refined and preferred the sort of company that never drank from tankards, or slurped their soup, or bent to some task in the garden. She was sure his table was always graced with the finest English crested china and that his servants would jump willingly from a cliff if he asked them to.

She'd noticed his large hands; his long, capable fingers were not callused. He probably hadn't known a hard day's work in his life.

Camille looked at her own hands. They were red and chafed from scrubbing grimy, ale-soaked floors at ungodly hours of the night and washing greasy platters night after night. They were certainly not the hands of a well-bred lady with a retinue of servants, nor would they ever be. Maybe once she had dreamed of that kind of life, long ago. She lowered them self-consciously to her sides.

She was in a fine mess now. She couldn't very well walk back to the tavern, so she would just have to find the stables—and then hope she could sweet-talk the stable boy into lending her a horse for the ride home. She could stable it down the street from the tavern until Nicholas could come and collect it; she knew the stable owner, a kind elderly man with young daughters who wouldn't ask questions. Harley had taught her how to ride, always had a fresh apple for her to give the horse.

Considering she was dressed like a street urchin', it wasn't going to be easy to convince the stable hand for the use of a horse. But it held less repugnance than facing Nicholas Branton again and asking him for help.

She walked around the side of the house, across a thick sweep of lush grass. Farther down the hillside, the river water glinted pearl-gray in the spring sunlight. Seeing a path, and the roofs of several whitewashed outbuildings, Camille headed that way.

3

Nick strode through the gardens thinking about the contract he'd signed on his father's deathbed. He would never forgive himself for being in England when it had all happened. If he'd come home sooner, perhaps he could have talked his father out of it. Perhaps he could have made a different decision. As it turned out, there was no time to discuss it, no time to find out why the betrothal had been arranged in the first place.

While he was in England, he'd received the letter from his father begging him to come home immediately. Caindale Branton never asked anyone for anything—let alone begged.

Nicholas had been on American soil only a few hours when he finally reached home and raced up to stairs to his father's darkened bedchamber. Genevieve, tears in her eyes, had caught him on the stairs.

"He's so sick, Nick. I've never seen him like this. He's grown worse in the past few days." She hugged Nick fiercely. "I'm glad your home. He keeps lapsing in and out of consciousness. He's been trying to tell me something, but I can't make any sense of it. He's delirious. He's been asking for you."

Nicholas was not prepared for the sight that greeted him. His father, a virile, forceful man, was weakly propped up on a mountain of pillows, his skin wan, his formidable frame withered. There were dark circles etched beneath his eyes. He looked so weak, so unlike himself.

Nicholas waited for his father's eyes to flutter open, sitting helplessly beside his bed, at a loss for words. His father motioned to the quill and ink on the bedside table and the papers sitting there.

His father's voice was weak; it slipped across the small space between them like a waning afternoon shadow. "You and I both know it should be Philip sitting in that chair."

Nicholas stiffened at the reference to his older brother, his father's golden boy, who had left years ago and had not been heard from since. Philip was four years his elder, and two brothers could not have been more unalike. Whereas Nicholas was dark like his mother, Philip had his father's head of golden hair, his father's angled chin and deep set blue eyes.

His father had lavished Philip with attention since the day he was born, had poured his heart and soul into grooming him to be his protégé. Philip had rewarded him by leaving home without so much as a backward glance, informing his father he didn't *want* the old man's business.

Nicholas couldn't imagine what his father had felt that day, *if* he'd felt anything at all. Caindale never expressed his emotions. He prided himself on his successes in the shipping business, and on his wealth, never on his family, unless it was Philip.

His father gasped for air, struggling to speak.

15

"But such is life. I don't know where my son is. I want you to sign that paper."

Nicholas was incredulous. "You're dying, and you're worried about *contracts*?"

"There isn't time. You must sign it and you must promise to honor it. I am giving you...the business, the estates, everything."

It was the last thing Nicholas expected. His voice was flat, neutral. "What's the catch, Caindale?" Nicholas had not called him father since he was a little boy.

"Ah, always the cynical one. Well, I suppose I am partly to blame for that. I cannot and will not say I'm sorry for who I am. I am the man I am."

It was the closest thing Nicholas had ever heard to an apology for his upbringing, the years of neglect he'd spent in Philip's shadow. Nicholas felt something foreign in his eyes—tears. He cleared his throat and quickly composed himself.

"We are alike in that respect, for I will not apologize for who *I* am. You always wanted me to be Philip. I am not Philip, nor will I ever be." Nicholas ground out the words, his dark jaw clenched.

Nicholas' father coughed, the spasms shaking his very bones.

"I must see you sign this paper before I die." He pulled the rope beside the bed, ringing the bell. Geoffry soon appeared.

"Geoffry can bear witness to your signature. It is all I ask. It makes you my official heir, giving you sole rights to everything I own. The business and the estates are in good shape. You will not have to worry about debt. If you manage things wisely, the business will be quite profitable for you."

Nicholas was torn between petty vengeance and guilt. He knew the business was profitable; he had made certain it would thrive, managing his father's foreign shipping interests only because there was no one else to do so. He had taken on those affairs at the age of seventeen.

Nicholas had grown up on the river, knew instinctively how to handle a boat since he was a lad. He'd spent time on a variety of vessels, fought the British on the open sea, even been promoted to Lieutenant. He knew how to handle a crew, knew how to wring from them exactly what was needed in a critical moment.

But the fact was he needed his father's wealth. It rankled. Not that he'd ever show it. He'd learned early not to reveal by his expression any inner thoughts or emotions, though his mouth suggested a capacity for humor. Some had told him he had a gambler's face, saved from sharpness by its strength.

He'd promised himself long-ago that he'd be a self-made and powerful man, more powerful than his father. He'd done things deliberately, with sweat and suffering. Smashed his fists into other men's faces, taken their blows on his own and on the hardened, trained muscles of his body. He'd shared stinking forecastles with men of every age and race, brutal men, broken men. He learned navigation on a tramp trader, fast sailing on an opium smuggler; he had learned the various merits of white oak and locust and cedar as apprentice to a builder. He knew which ships would have speed and which would carry the greatest cargo.

Still, no matter what he did, his father never acknowledged any of it. Nicholas knew he would never hear any praise from his father's lips for his accomplishments, nor did he expect it. Yet

18

Philip, who had once deserted his post as a lieutenant during a battle with a Spanish corvette, still had his father's admiration.

His brother's career in the navy and been short and inglorious. He'd come home after his discharge and rifled through a vast amount of Caindale's money before Caindale put a stop to it. That was probably why Philip had left in such a huff; no one had ever denied Philip anything.

For a moment, Nicholas thought about refusing his father's wishes, pride swelling in his chest. He was a self-made man; he hadn't ever needed his father's guidance. Then he looked at the bitter, old man before him, who would die alone.

It was true he wasn't Philip, but by signing that paper, Nicholas had some control over his future. He could run the business completely on his own terms. And if he didn't, what would happen to his high-spirited sister, Genevieve?

He reached out, took the quill, and penned his name at the bottom of the document. Geoffry signed his own name and left them alone. Nicholas looked up and met his father's eyes. There was more said between them in that moment then in any other when they had exchanged words.

"Now leave me to die in peace."

Nicholas stood, took one last, long glance at his father, bowed his head, and left. Inside he felt like screaming; he felt like crying; he felt angry as hell. But his father wanted none of his pity, his unexpected sorrow, his anger. He had never wanted him as a son. Nicholas had always known it, deep down in a part of his soul he had closed off long ago.

A few hours later, his father died. It was not until after the funeral, after his father was buried in the Branton family crypt that Nicholas looked over the contract. Turned out, his father had the last laugh. Nicholas had been made sole owner of his father's business and estates, but at a heady price.

Nicholas had almost balled the document up with his fists and thrown it into the fire crackling in the hearth, for his father still controlled him from the grave. He would have to do the one thing he's sworn never to do again. He would have to marry, and quickly, or he would lose everything, everything he had helped to build up.

If he did not marry, it would all be held in trust for his brother and Nicholas would be banned from the property. His home. Nicholas had no doubt that Caindale's attorney, Hugh Harcourt, a barrel-shaped man with the temperament of a bull, would see fit to make sure that Nicholas would lose it all if he refused to go through with the marriage. He had no doubt Harcourt would gleefully escort him from his home, the home he had grown up in as a child.

Nicholas stood on the front porch now, his mood angry and vengeful. Through the moss-draped oaks, he caught a glimpse of his betrothed, the urchin', and stepped up his pace. Had Caindale been mad?

4

The path threaded its way through magnificent, well-tended gardens, the like of which Camille had never seen. Clusters of flowers dotted the walks like miniature rainbows; carved cherubic statues and waterfalls added to the enchantment of the setting.

The graded terrace, walled with orange-red azaleas, gave way to alcoves of tea roses, daffodils, floribundas, and crape myrtle.

Camille became almost dizzy as she moved quickly along intersecting walkways trimmed with boxwoods and lime-green Chinese cane. For a brief moment, she wondered what it would be like to be the lady of the house, to have such wonderful gardens to walk in every day. The zesty fragrance of sweet olive, juniper, and lemon verbena assailed her as she walked the paths, which were shadowed by the arms of great moss-draped oaks that were hundreds of years old.

Eventually, she came to a secluded spot on the bank of the river. *Now what?* she thought. Impossibly, the outbuildings seemed to be even farther away now. Her sense of direction had never been her strongest asset. She stood looking out at the river, trying to get her bearings.

A great lump rose in her throat as she thought of everything that could have been—if only her parents had lived. From what her uncle had told her, they weren't rich people. But that didn't matter to Camille. It never had.

She was sure they were kind, kinder than her uncle, and she was sure they had married for love. She didn't remember too much about them but once in awhile she had flashbacks, memories from long ago, when she was a little girl.

Camille watched the crimson and gold-flecked sunset. Getting home was a minor inconvenience, she mused, compared to the thought of spending a lifetime with Nicholas Branton. *Ill-bred, coarse-mannered horse's ass!*

She sighed, knowing now that she wouldn't have to. She would have to find a way to deal with her uncle's wrath, but even that was preferable to....

"Lose your way, urchin'?" a deep, masculine voice said from behind her. She turned to find Nicholas Branton staring at her, leaning lazily against the wide base of an old oak tree, his muscular arms crossed over his wide chest. His chest was nearly as wide as the tree. He had narrow hips, but there was no mistaking the powerful muscles in his thighs. Dear Lord, his black breeches were so tight they were unseemly. Camille looked away, hoping he hadn't caught the blush rising to her cheeks.

"Ain't none of yer business, but yes. I was lookin' for the stables."

"Going to steal a horse?"

Camille clenched her teeth. Just because she wasn't dressed like a wealthy socialite didn't mean she was a thief. Of course, she *had* been thinking of stealing a horse, but only temporarily....

Horse's ass. "I ain't no thief, mister. I just want to get home afore dark."

"I must insist you stay for dinner."

She turned to face him, squaring her small shoulders.

"I told you, I ain't stayin' for dinner. Ain't got no cause to stay for dinner."

"You sure you won't reconsider?"

"I wouldn't stay if you paid me a hundred dollars in gold."

"You leave me no choice then." Nicholas removed his burgundy overcoat, laid it on the ground at his feet, and came toward her.

Before she could utter a sound, she felt a pair of strong arms about her waist, lifting her as if she were a feather adrift on the wind, dragging her toward the river's edge.

"Put me down!" her voice rose hysterically and she began frantically kicking her legs and arms, all to no avail. He carried her easily, pinned snugly against his side, then plopped her unceremoniously into the water.

Shock. Pure, cold shock. Camille felt herself sinking and began flailing her limbs. Dear God, she would drown, she was sure of it! She couldn't make heads or tails of the bottom or the surface.

Just when she felt sure her lungs would burst, the water rippled and splashed and she felt strong arms about her waist again, bringing her gently to the surface.

Nicholas pulled her out of the water and sat on the bank, cradling her small form against his broad chest. The sun was now a hazy ball of orange over the horizon and Camille coughed and sputtered, desperately seeking its warmth.

"Urchin', it would seem we are both in need of a bath now."

"My nnnn...name is Camille," she gritted out, her teeth chattering. "Not urchin'."

She reached up, belatedly realizing she'd lost her cap and her hair had tumbled down her shoulders. She felt like a river rat and she couldn't stop shivering.

His eyes narrowed as he took in the sun-kissed mass of wet, tangled hair, the creamy, smooth complexion of her skin, which had been hidden from him in his study. Her small fingers clutched at his shirt, unconsciously seeking the heat of his skin beneath.

"You're trembling," he said. "Do I frighten you?"

"I'm ccc...cold, you witling. And I cccc...can't sww...swim!" she said, her eyes dazed.

"Bloody hell." Nicholas regretted his hasty actions; he'd had no idea she couldn't swim. His sister could; but then again, his sister wasn't a typical female—she'd had to keep up with him.

"You'll feel better after a warm bath and dinner."

"Yer plan all along?" she said, gritting her teeth. They stood and he retrieved his burgundy jacket, draping it over her shoulders. She was small, and the coat hung on her shoulders. He led her along the path back to the house, his hand at the small of her back.

"That weren't fair, mister." She shivered again, this time not knowing if it was from the cold, wet rags she was tangled in or from the touch of his warm skin, the strange, uncertain way those gold eyes had touched her face, her hair. She had the feeling he was a complicated man, a man it would take a lifetime to know. A man to *avoid.*

Back in the main hall, they were greeted by Geoffry. He showed not the slightest hint of surprise at Camille's disheveled appearance.

"Geoffry, see that Miss Hardison is comfortably settled and a bath drawn," Nicholas said. "She had a rather unfortunate encounter with the river."

"Yes Sir. Right away sir," Geoffry said, disappearing into the cavernous halls of the house.

Genevieve soon appeared. She gave her brother a disapproving look then took Camille's hand. Nicholas sauntered off, leaving matters in her capable hands.

"You must be dreadfully cold and wet. Follow me, and we'll get you out of those wet rag...clothes. I'm so happy you're staying."

"I ain't happy 'bout it," Camille replied. She felt her anger rise anew. Nicholas had won this round, but she vowed the next would be hers. Why was he being so stubborn? Why was he insisting on her staying? She wondered belatedly if he'd ever dunked any of his other lady callers in the river. She had a funny feeling she wasn't the first. She could just imagine them all bobbing up and down in their hooped skirts and petticoats like so much forgotten driftwood.

Perhaps he was simply mad, his mind unbalanced…and that was why he wasn't married.

She followed Genevieve up the wide, carpeted staircase, her wet shoes making ungodly sucking sounds. Candles in their brass sconces flickered haughtily on the portraits of present and long-dead Brantons, all of whom seemed to mock her from the shadows.

5

Camille looked around the guestroom. It was very tastefully decorated with a hand-carved four-poster bed and matching rosewood armoire, a dressing table with a bowl of freshly picked wildflowers, and a large gold-leaf framed mirror.

There were yellow silken draperies on the windows, and a low fire burned in the Egyptian marble fireplace. A petite crystal chandelier hung from the medallioned ceiling.

Above the bed was a portrait of a young woman with large fawn-colored eyes and a devilish smile on her face. With her mane of gently curling, lustrous black hair, high cheekbones, and fine porcelain skin, the woman looked very much like Genevieve.

The mansion was certainly an enchanting place, and Camille would have liked to explore it. It was imposing with its statuesque Greek columns, and it lay near the river in fertile, flat land created by centuries of overflow.

Camille had heard that some planters made huge fortunes in only a few years; they filled their homes with imported furnishings, made the European grand tour, and concerned themselves with the finer things in life. Camille wondered what the Brantons had built their fortune on, for she hadn't seen any slaves in the outer buildings; they looked vacant. If she had, she would've run home. She'd seen the horrible looks of despair and fear on the faces of slaves being sold at auctions. It was the vilest evil Camille could think of, the most horrible separation of human beings from the people they loved.

There was a knock on the door.

"Come in," Camille said, unaccustomed to privacy.

A plump servant entered, followed by a slew of others carrying buckets of hot water.

"Welcome to Legacy Oaks. I'm to help ye with yer bath. Name's Lucille, but everyone in these parts just calls me plain Lucy."

"Name's Camille."

"I gathered that much. Lordy, look at ye, dear. It's gonna take some scrubbin'. How'd ye get so wet and dirty?"

"I'd rather not say," Camille replied.

"That'll ne'er do, ne'er do," Lucy said. "Follow me."

Camille followed Lucy through a door to a small adjoining room with a curved, high-back tin tub, which the servants filled with hot water and the most delicious-smelling soaps. They quickly went back to their other duties.

"I suggest ye strip down and start lathering up; it'll chase away the chill. Lordy, but you'll catch your death running about in wet clothes."

A hot bath suddenly appealed to Camille after a day that was anything but normal; she rarely had the luxury of one and she didn't feel like catching her death of chill, so she stripped off her grubby clothing and shyly climbed into the tub.

There was no formal bathing area in the upstairs rooms of the tavern; most of the time, she had to make due with a cloth, a crude chunk of soap, and a chipped porcelain bowl filled with cold water when she washed in the mornings.

While she was here, it was the least Nicholas could do for her, considering this whole unfortunate incident was his fault. Besides, her clothes stank to high heaven like dank river water.

She sank down into the tub, letting the steam soak into her pores as her hair tumbled over the side of the tub, nearly touching the floor. Lucy picked up her clothes.

As Camille scrubbed off the filth, she began to feel like her old self again. Lucy left her for a short while, shaking her head and threatening to return with a lot more soap.

Camille felt a small ache in her chest and tried to ignore it. She'd never felt so alone, so out of place, so lost. Her uncle had expected her to be jubilant about marrying a wealthy man. He'd laughed at her when she told him she would rather marry for love.

"You ain't gonna get any offers for marriage, sweetie," he said. "And if you do, he ain't gonna be no gentleman." She wouldn't tell her uncle about Christopher, an English sea captain and one of the few tavern patrons who'd ever shown her respect.

He was tall, with blonde hair, and fair to look upon. She'd quickly fallen in love with him, though he'd only visited the tavern on two occasions. He was kind, and promised to write to her from his next port. And *he* wanted to marry her. He'd told her so before he left. He'd said she'd make any man a first-rate wife, then winked, his blue eyes bright, and asked her to wait for him.

He wasn't arrogant, or complicated, or dark, like Nicholas Branton. His eyes weren't a heated gold-brown, and maybe his shoulders weren't as wide as Nicholas'...why was she comparing the two men?

The more she thought about her uncle, and about Nicholas dumping her in the river, the angrier she became. A string of vile tavern oaths would have left her mouth at exactly that moment if Lucy hadn't returned.

"Lucy...okay if'n I call you Lucy?"

"You certainly can, missy," Lucy giggled. "Master Branton is sure gonna be tickled 'bout this change!"

What change? Dear God, all the filth was gone. She couldn't hide behind it anymore. Still, Camille took the chunky, rose-colored soaps and another washcloth offered by Lucy. She couldn't help but run her fingers over the smooth soaps, deeply inhaling their pretty, feminine fragrance.

"Why do you hide yourself in such rags, girl? Lordy, but I never would have believed this!" Lucy was a talker, and from what Camille could guess, a harmless gossip. She liked her immediately.

Lucy began washing Camille's hair. "Why, girl, your hair is as fine as spun gold!"

"What's he like, Lucy?"

"You mean Nick? He's a fine one, that one. Been a bit of a rogue since he was knee-high to a musquito. Always was gettin' into some scrape or 'nother. Not a'feared of nothin', that one. Doesn't mince his words neither, not by a jugful. But ne'er sassy to me, no.

"See, I raised him since he was a babe, he and his sister and brother. His father was always off on business. His mother died when he was young. Wouldn't dare raise his voice to ol' Lucy." She continued to wash and rinse Camille's hair. "Well, I think yer as clean as can be now," Lucy said.

Camille rose out of the water and was wrapped in a thick, soft green dressing robe. They returned to the bedchamber and Camille sat in the chair before the dressing table.

"Who's that?" Camille asked, looking at the portrait again. Lucy was silent for a moment.

"That was Caroline, their mother."

"I can see where Genevieve gets her fine looks." *And Nicholas too, for that matter*, Camille thought.

"This was her room, you know. She liked it because it looked out toward the river...and the ruins of the ol' abbey. She used to tell me it gave her some sort of odd peace." Camille sensed that she wanted to say more about the woman in the portrait, but she didn't.

"I'll send Genevieve in soon. Sure enough, that child has something you can wear. Lord, she has more fancy clothes than the Queen of England."

"Thanks, Lucy. I don't need to borrow nothin, though. I'll just put my own clothes back on when they dry."

Lucy laughed and slapped her rounded thigh. "Child that would be a sight. Your clothes done fell apart. You can't wear that robe to dinner neither. You'll borrow one of Miss Genevieve's nice gowns. Now, you just relax."

"But...."

"Gracious, sweetie, a little southern hospitality never hurt no one."

Hospitality? More like conspiracy.

The stout woman left Camille alone in the big, silent room. She dried off, put the robe on, and crossed the floor to the window, looking out at the shadows of the great moss-draped oaks and the silhouette of riders along the levee.

The spring rains had come down hard for the past few days, and the river had begun to swell. She knew from personal experience just how cold it was.

By the time her hair had dried, one of the servants arrived to help Camille finish her toilette, sweeping up her hair and letting a few wisps fall around her face. There was another knock on the door. This was getting ridiculous, all this pampering!

Why were they going to the trouble? Why was Genevieve being so nice to her? And how was she going to explain herself to her uncle when she returned to the tavern looking this way?

"Come in," Camille said. Genevieve's eyes sparkled impishly as she handed Camille something to wear.

"What happened to the grubby little urchin'?" She laughed. "I'm glad to see you out of those wet clothes, Camille."

Genevieve appeared to be waiting for an explanation, but when none was forthcoming, she said, "I brought a chemise and petticoats. I made them myself and they've never been worn. I'd also like you to have this...I think we're probably about the same size." Camille looked at the beautiful white muslin dress. Now she had no choice but to wear it.

She didn't want her life complicated by marriage, complicated by a man like Nicholas Branton. Why was everyone being so stubborn about it? She was a common tavern maid, for God's sake, not a desirable socialite. She wasn't even beautiful. Her uncle had told her over and over that she was 'passable.' She had nothing to offer the man! How in the world had this betrothal come about?

A faint smile curved her lips. All was not lost. She might look like a lady after she put the dress on, but that didn't mean she had to act like one. All she had to do was get through dinner, get home, and find some way to return the pretty clothes to Genevieve.

A servant helped her to dress. Camille's stomach was grumbling—she hadn't eaten a thing all day. Not that she could. Every time she thought of marriage to Nicholas Branton, a vision of a lecherous old man with rotting teeth and whiskey breath popped into her head. She certainly hadn't expected him to be so...virile. She knew instinctively that the man was definitely not husband-material.

"Miss, why is you bein' so nice? Why all the pamperin'?"

"Please, call me Genevieve. And why shouldn't I be nice to you? You act as if I'm breaking the law by showing you a kindness."

"Well, it's just that, folks of yer station don't usually treat someone like me with...kindness."

Genevieve grasped Camille's hand.

"Let's forget our stations for a while, shall we? That doesn't matter anyway. I just want to get to know you a little better."

Camille nodded shyly.

39

"Okay, but I can't stay." Camille suddenly felt sad. Here was a kind girl who felt like a friend, but Camille knew it wouldn't last. They came from different worlds. But she didn't have too many friends.

Genevieve winked. The transformation complete, they left the room, made their way down the hall, and descended the stairs together, Camille's heart hammering in her chest.

Nicholas Branton, dry and shaven, was dressed in a dark overcoat, trousers, and a crisp white shirt. He was standing at the bottom of the staircase waiting for them, one arm casually hung over the banister. His eyes, darker now and tinged with gold, traveled leisurely over her form; they lingered on the swell of her breasts and her slim hips. *He wasn't smiling.*

6

Nicholas took her arm in his, but said nothing, his lips drawn into a hard line. They walked down the wide hallways over pine-heart floors so polished that Camille was nearly blinded. A low murmur of voices drifted toward them.

"We have guests this evening," he said, arching a dark brow and his eyes probed hers.

Camille smiled demurely. "That's just dee-lightful," she quipped. She thought she detected a slight grimace on his much-too-handsome face.

The dining room was open and airy, the walls papered in a creamy gold-flocked pattern. Carved, high-back chairs surrounded a

42

gleaming oblong table that sparkled with silver and fine porcelain. Candles flickered softly on the table and the mantle above the marble hearth, adding to the warmth of the room.

"Martha, Harold, may I present Miss Camille Hardison," Nicholas said. "The Quinns are frequent visitors from a nearby mansion and were good friends of my mother's," Nicholas explained.

The pair stood. Harold was a pleasant-looking, red-cheeked man with a rather round face. Martha was a plump, flamboyant woman with garishly red-orange hair who was wearing an ample boa feather around her shoulders. Camille had never seen so many feathers on a human. She smiled warmly.

"Howdy do," Camille said.

She felt Nicholas stiffen beside her.

"Why this is a delight," Martha said. "A lady guest tonight, Nicholas?"

"I ain't no lady."

Martha laughed loudly, the blue and yellow feathers of her boa quivering with the effort. "Well, my dear, and Thank God for that. Being a lady is quite frankly overrated."

"Camille is my fiancé. We are…betrothed." Nicholas hastily seated Camille between Genevieve and Martha before seating himself at the head of the table. There was stunned silence.

"Mr. Branton is confused…I ain't agreed to marry no one."

As cold tomato and cucumber soup was served, Martha cleared her throat awkwardly and asked Camille what family she was from.

"I ain't no blue-blood, if that's what you mean," Camille said. "My mother and father died a long time back. I work in my uncle's tavern in the city—perhaps you've heard of it? The Black Garter?" She looked at Nicholas. "I…got soaked in the river and that's why I'm wearin' one of Miss Genny's gowns." Careful not to spill anything on the dress, Camille deliberately picked up the bowl of soup with her fingers, brought it to her mouth, and began slurping loudly. She'd seen plenty of patrons at the tavern do exactly that, and most often, if you offered them utensils, they glared at you.

"Oh, my dear, I certainly didn't mean to offend. We're from England originally. My great grandfather was a footman. But that didn't stop Harold from marrying me.

"You see, Harold was a very distant relation to some Prince but he defied his father's wishes and married me anyway. No, we're not pretentious people. Life is too short for that." She paused to take a breath and continued.

"Dear me, but after that battle in the harbor, we weren't very popular in these parts, being English and all. And it was certainly humiliating for England when our troops, which had just vanquished that little water rat Napoleon, were defeated by a bunch of disorganized, scraggly Americans. But we consider ourselves more American than English, and those troops had heart."

"You'll have to excuse my wife. Talks too much about wars and politics and things that don't concern her."

"Why, certainly they concern me," Martha replied. "There isn't a reason on earth why a woman *shouldn't* be concerned about such things."

Harold smiled complacently and sighed.

"I think if she could, she'd put on a soldier's uniform and march off to fight. Thank the Good Lord in Heaven that soldiers don't wear feathers."

Much to Camille's surprise, Martha picked up her bowl of soup and began slurping.

"Yes, I like this. It's rather fun." Harold rolled his eyes.

Camille was too stunned to speak. She slurped her way through the rest of the meal, deliberately ignoring the shiny utensils by her plate, licking her fingers noisily, barely grunting in response to questions. She listened as they spoke of Nicholas' father. She thought she saw something flash in Nicholas' eyes at the mention of his name, but it was gone as quickly as it had come. They inquired after his young daughters, Arabelle and Damaris, who were now abed.

Daughters? The thought didn't have time to digest itself.

Genevieve talked of upcoming soirees and the balls she would be attending, while Martha suggested the names of handsome, eligible bachelors she might consider as husband material. Genevieve then related the faults of each in painstaking detail.

Camille was beginning to panic. Despite her ill manners, she had yet to shock them. She looked up once or twice to find Nicholas' eyes on her, but they were unreadable.

The meal was nearly over. Unexpectedly, Camille recalled a similar room, fine china, her father and mother laughing together. Her father was flinging food and her mother was flinging it right back. Her head started to ache. The memories were always so vivid, but her uncle insisted they were just the fancies of a poor girl, nothing more.

He'd told her many times she couldn't possibly have any memories of them; she was so young when they'd died, and they'd never lived in such a grand manner.

Dear God, what did she have to do to shock these people? Suddenly it came to her. Nicholas was rising from the table, turning to go. She had so thoroughly disgusted him he hadn't even excused himself politely. Wasn't that what these types did? Excused themselves from the table properly?

Camille slid some peas onto her spoon and angled her wrist. With all the deftness and grace she could muster, she sent the peas flying, hitting Nicholas square in his masculine backside.

He stopped but did not turn around, peas rolling ignobly at his feet. The room had gone quiet. Camille smiled. She couldn't help it.

"Madame, did you just fling *peas* at me?"

Geoffry, who had been standing by the doorway with a linen napkin draped over his arm, laughed loudly. He quickly recovered himself, clearing his throat. Harold and his overdressed wife joined in.

No! They weren't supposed to be laughing! They were supposed to be appalled, disgusted, speechless! They were supposed to think she was ill-mannered, crude, and atrociously behaved!

Nicholas' deep voice cut through the banter. He still had his back to her.

"Madame, you are worse than my own daughters. I will see you, alone, in my study. Now." With that, he strode out of the room, never questioning that she should follow him.

Harold was the first to recover. He wiped at his watering eyes.

"This has been the most entertaining evening I've had out in a very long time. Isn't that right, Martha? You ask me, his backside needed a good pea-slinging!"

Martha rolled her eyes and laughed.

"Marvelous, my dear. Dinner parties are usually so stuffy, people talking about the weather, the latest blight to their crops, or some such boring thing. Honestly!" She turned serious for a moment and grasped Camille's hand warmly.

"I've known Nicholas for a long time. He wasn't always so hard. His mother and I were great friends. And if you ask me"—she leaned over the table conspiratorially—"he's been much too serious since his first wife.... Well anyway, My God, but Marlena certainly never would have done *that*." She looked faintly disapproving when she spoke of Marlena.

"She never did anything that wasn't to her benefit…leaving two daughters behind…."

"Yes, a great tragedy, but that's enough, Martha," Harold said, more sternly this time.

"Tragedy, humph."

Camille was too shocked to speak. Good God, were they all daft? *She* was supposed to be shocking them, not the other way around! *First wife?*

She stood, excused herself, and followed Nicholas down the hallway to his study. She didn't follow him because he expected her to but because she needed to tell him that he couldn't order her about like one of his servants! She didn't belong to him; she would never belong to him!

7

Camille opened the door to the study and stomped in.

"Close the door, madame. I would converse in private."

Another order. She ignored his request. "You are the most arrogant, pompous, atrociously behaved gentleman I have ever met and this whole arrangement is utterly preposterous."

He stepped out of the shadows.

"What did you say?"

Camille flushed, her mind gone suddenly blank with fear.

"I said it was a foolish idee..."

"That's not exactly what you said, is it my dear?"

She'd just slipped up royally. She smoothed her dress, clenching and unclenching her small hands at her sides, and began pacing.

He continued to lean against the massive mahogany desk, his powerful arms crossed in front of him, calmly studying her. He removed his dinner jacket and walked to the sideboard.

"Would you like a brandy, Miss Hardison? You are obviously an educated lady. Yet you act as if you were raised in a barn. Care to explain?"

Camille faltered. "Not in a barn. A tavern. And no thank you." She cleared her throat nervously. "I mean no thank you to the brandy." There was no avoiding the truth now.

"As far as an explanation, it's simple. I...do you have any dreams, Mr. Branton?" He looked momentarily stunned as he poured brandy from a crystal liqueur decanter into a glass, took a sip, and then set his glass down on the desk. "Dreams are the useless fantasies of fools."

He moved to the window and laced his arms behind his back, staring out at the darkened sky, latticed with swollen storm clouds.

"Well, you can afford not to dream," Camille said quietly. "I...I do not wish to marry...for the wrong reasons."

"Nor do I, Miss Hardison."

She sighed with relief, a bit too loudly. She did not see the hard frown that crossed his features. She studied the broad expanse of his back, his wide shoulders, his lean hips.

"Were the ill manners and...charming...speech deliberate?" he asked.

"I... Yes. I hoped you would take one look at me, be appalled by my manners, and send me away."

"I wish it were that simple, Miss Hardison, but it's not. Logic...doesn't play into it."

He continued to present his back. "I'm curious though; with the improvement of your station through marriage to me, I'm surprised someone like you wouldn't jump at the chance."

Someone like you? Camille fumed.

"It's simple," she replied. "As for *someone like me* jumping at the chance to marry *someone like you*, well, I wish to marry for love, not money, Mr. Branton. And despite the fact that my 'station' is lower in life than yours, it would seem I have the higher ideals."

He turned and pinned her in his dark gaze. "Do your higher ideals include lying about who and what you are, Miss Hardison, to get what you want?"

Camille blushed. "I did what I needed to do. Nobody was hurt. I knew you would call it off the moment you saw me, the moment you heard me speak. It just took a little bit longer than I expected."

"Who said anything about calling it off?"

Camille felt as if someone had sucked all of the air out of the dimly lit room.

"You can't be serious...after everything...."

"Oh, I'm serious, Miss Hardison. In fact, I see no reason why the ceremony can't be performed posthaste. Marriage is, after all, just a piece of paper, and it would be a quiet, simple ceremony with no frills. No planning would be necessary."

"Posthaste? Are you mad, sir?" Frantic, she decided to humor him. "And where might we find a preacher at such short notice?"

"Harold is a preacher. He's performed quite a few impromptu weddings over the years."

Camille sat down on high-backed chair. "Good God, you are daft as a donkey. That's it, isn't it? You're mad? That's why you aren't married, that's why your first wife...."

She stopped, his eyes like dark sparks.

"You would be wise not to mention my wife…ever again."

Camille nodded her head slowly, feeling like a caged animal.

"We don't need to make this complicated. The last thing I want or need is a wife."

"What are you saying? I don't understand. You said you had no wish to marry…."

"It was my father's dying wish that I marry you. I doubt I will ever understand his reasoning, but I intend to honor his wishes. It will be perfectly legal—I will be your lawfully wedded husband; you will be my 'loving' wife. No one has to know that the marriage is a sham. What I am saying, madame, is that you do not need to share my bed. It will be a marriage in name only." He paused. "Unless, at some point, you find you cannot resist. Women tend to leave my bed

heartily satisfied."

Camille felt the hot blush on her cheeks deepening. "How noble

of you, sir. But let me assure you, I have no desire to…I would never

find pleasure in your bed."

Camille had never been with a man, so she didn't really know

what pleasures were to be had, but he didn't have to know that.

She'd heard enough tales from her best friend Meagan, who also

worked at the tavern, to know that it was generally the man who

found pleasure, not the woman. And she hadn't even known his

father, so why would he wish the match between them? None of it

made any sense. How had her uncle known this arrogant man's

father?

Camille thought of her childhood dreams, the lavish wedding

she'd always wanted, a doting husband, small children to love and

cherish...saw them all slipping away the same way so many other

things in her life had slipped away.

"That is most fortunate," he finally said, "for I have no desire to sleep with a common tavern maid who's been pawed by more men than she can count on both hands."

Dear God, but he was crude, and his words stung. She felt tears brimming but thrust her chin up. Well, what could she expect? Her uncle had always told her that no well-bred gentleman would ever desire her, not even as a mistress. Mistresses were exotic, sultry, and much desired. And she wasn't about to correct his assumption about her morals.

"Fortunate indeed," she said, "for I have no desire to sleep with a horse's ass. Tavern maids and horses' asses do not make a good match."

In the darkness, she did not see the sensual smile tugging at his lips.

"Touché, madame. We understand each other. We are completely unsuited. I prefer a more sophisticated lady and you, I imagine, dream of a gentleman with higher ideals, one who is quite out of your reach. You are obviously not sophisticated and I am by no means a gentleman with higher ideals. Nor will I ever be."

Camille did not raise her eyes to look at him.

"Yes," she said quietly, thinking of how he had carelessly tossed her in the river to get his way. "We understand each other. But I haven't consented to this match. Why should I marry you?"

"Because, my dear, you have no choice." The pair turned, startled, to see Penley Hardison filling out the doorway to the study like a crude blob of jelly. He stepped inside without waiting for an invitation. Nicholas wondered just how long he had been eavesdropping.

"I came as soon as I heard you'd left for Legacy Oaks, my dear." He shook his fat finger at Camille. "Meagan told me what you were about." Camille couldn't believe Meagan had betrayed her trust. She stared suspiciously at Penley.

The rain and wind had played havoc with his appearance. His single strand of limp gray hair was wrapped around his bald head in a most unbecoming manner; his garish clothes were wrinkled and stretched tautly across his ample paunch. Gaudy, gold rings danced clumsily on his fingers, catching the light from the fire in the hearth.

"I don't believe I've had the pleasure." Nicholas' acerbic tone was lost on the man.

Penley walked over to Nicholas and extended his hand. Nicholas' arms remained crossed over his chest, his eyes hard and unyielding.

"Penley Hardison. I knew your father quite well, quite well indeed."

Nicholas looked at him with disdain. "I can't imagine what you and Caindale had in common, though I can guess it had something to do with gambling. My father had a penchant for that sort of thing. And I'm sure you were eager to take his coin." Penley drew up his short frame.

"I came to make sure you would honor your word, sir."

"I fully intend to honor my word—for the sole purpose of fulfilling my father's last wishes."

Penley's boldness returned. "See that you do."

The look that crossed Nicholas' features was cat-like and murderous. Camille jumped in.

"Excuse me, but we are discussing *my* future, and I have decided against this marriage, should anyone care to notice."

"I would have a word with my niece," Penley said.

"Certainly. I've had my fill of her company—as well as yours," Nicholas replied, leaving the two alone.

Camille tried to stand, but Penley had crossed the room and pushed her forcefully back into her seat. He lowered his voice.

"You ungrateful chit! What do you think you are doing? I took you in, fed you, clothed you. I would see you comfortably settled, and this is how you show your gratitude? By trying to get it called off? Why in God's name would you prefer the tavern to all this wealth?" He gestured with his stubby arms and fat fingers at the room and luxury surrounding them.

"You never wanted me, uncle. I have clearly been a burden to you since I was a child. You've made that clear. Everything you've given me has been given begrudgingly, and you have never spared extra for my needs." Camille thought of Christopher's smiling eyes, his kindness, her promise to wait for him, and her courage returned.

"There is nothing you can do to make me agree to marriage with that man."

Penley rocked back on his heels, scratching his rotund chin. His eyes were as cruel and black as a raven's.

"It's true I never wanted to take you in. Why would I want a mouth to feed, a sniggling brat to deal with? But what else could I do? Leave you to the streets? You are...kin."

"Come now, uncle, you've never done anything that wasn't to your benefit. Though I am grateful you gave me a roof over my head, I've had to earn my keep. Since I was twelve, I've fallen into bed every night exhausted from the tasks you set me. I never had a childhood. As far as I'm concerned, we're even. I'll say it again. I will not marry him."

Penley leaned over her, placing one stout arm on each side of her, forcing her back in the seat. He lowered his voice so only she could hear.

"That's where you're wrong, my dear. How do you think I got Meagan to spill her guts? Even now Meletios waits outside in the carriage. His knuckles are still sore from the beating he gave her, but he will gladly use them again to convince you of the error of your ways."

Camille paled. Meletios was a huge man, a well-known thug her uncle hired out when he had gambling debts to collect. He would do anything for the right price. Her uncle, in fact, was not a poor man. He owned a string of taverns. He profited from a lot of unsavory activities. And those he employed usually suffered for it.

"It's your choice. You can get married, in fact, why not tonight, or you can come with us and be convinced what's best for you. You are grown now; I don't have any further obligation to you."

Sweet God, did Nicholas know about Meletios? He had seemed generally surprised to discover the man eavesdropping at the study door was her Uncle Penley, so maybe he didn't know. Nicholas didn't seem to be the kind of man who would allow a woman to be beaten, but she didn't know him at all. And he was determined to wed her. Perhaps he knew of her uncle's threats and simply didn't care.

Camille shivered. She tried to keep the tremor out of her voice. "There will be no need for that, uncle. Though I must wonder at the urgency. There must be something in it for you."

"It's a business transaction, m'dear, the details of which do not concern you. Caindale needed to settle a debt with me. Now, I will have your answer." Penley stepped away and waited, tapping his boot-clad foot. Camille stood up. She mustered as much dignity as she could.

"Give Meletios my condolences," she managed, her throat a tight, achy knot from the tears that threatened to spill down her cheeks. "For he will not have an opportunity to beat another woman this evening." Camille hoped he would never have another opportunity.

"I knew you would come to your senses," Penley replied. "I'll inform Mr. Branton, and the others, of your decision. Now chin up, girl."

Penley strode toward the door, arrogance in his stride.

"Uncle." He stopped but did not turn around.

"This isn't over," Camille said softly. "One day you'll pay for the way you've mistreated me...for what you've done to Meagan. And the other girls." Thunder clapped outside and jagged streaks of lightning cavorted in the dark sky.

He laughed. "You're a bold wench, Camille. But that's all you'll ever be. Somebody's stupid wench." He paused. "If it wasn't for our blood relation, I would've humbled you too, long ago, with the prick between my legs."

He strode out of the study chuckling and closed the door, closeting her in the lonely darkness with her thoughts. She sat down, feeling weak and emotionally drained.

She stared out the window for what seemed an eternity, listening to the staccato tapping of rain on the roof, for the storm clouds had opened up like flowers in the spring. Exhausted and defeated, she pulled the pins from her hair, letting them drop to the floor. She was tired of the charade. She had lost. In that moment, it was as if all her dreams drifted away like parchment on a stiff winter wind. An aching sadness settled over her soul, warring with her anger. And Nicholas was to blame for agreeing to this match. Camille had truly never hated anyone as much before, not even her uncle, until that moment.

"I see no reason to wait. Are you ready then?" Camille hadn't heard Nicholas come in. She continued to look at the floor, determined not to show him the hurt in her soul.

"You will...not change your mind and demand your husbandly rights?" she asked.

"As I stated before, madame, we are completely unsuited. I do not desire you in the least, nor would I take an unwilling woman to my bed."

She stood on shaky legs. "I will agree to this marriage...this sham...with the condition that we never share a bed," she replied. "As for the ceremony, I suggest we get it over with as quickly as possible. I'm tired. I wish to go to bed. Alone," she quickly added, heading toward the door. Just as she was about to reach it, he barred her exit with his arm. He was too close now, and she found the faint scent of brandy clinging to his masculine form not unpleasant. She stared at his chest.

"Miss Hardison, I have a condition or two of my own."

"You would demand more of me? Pray tell, Mr. Branton, what might those conditions be?"

Rain and wind hammered against the sides of the house and the roof. Her heart hammered in her chest. She knew she was baiting him. Despite the fear that leapt in her soul she did it anyway.

"Everything that is mine is at your disposal, of course. The stables, so there is no need to *steal* a horse, the seamstress should you desire a new wardrobe. Whatever you may need. As my wife, you shall receive a handsome allowance every month, to use as you see fit.

"Therefore, from this day forward, you will not slave tables in a tavern. All I ask is that you act the part of lady. As it does for all women, acting seems to come naturally for you."

Her shoulders came up. Too late, she realized what her pride had cost her. He was so close she could feel the long, lean hardness of him, the contours of his muscled thighs pressed against the soft, feminine curves of her own. As if he sensed her discomfort, he moved even closer.

"The other condition?" she asked quickly, alarmed by the hard heat of his body.

His warm breath brushed her ear as he bent closer to her face and sent dangerous shivers down her spine. His voice was a gruff whisper. "In future, urchin', you will refrain from flinging peas at my backside."

"Oh, if I must," she whispered. Nicholas almost laughed.

He backed away, allowing her to precede him into the hallway. He walked behind her, his hand gently guiding her, his large palm pressed into the curve of her back. The sight that greeted Camille in the sun parlor made her gasp in surprise.

8

Josephine Huxley was, as usual, impeccably dressed. She wore a white muslin walking dress with a spencer of lilac sarcenet, diamonds glittered on her long, graceful fingers, and her silvery-grey hair was swept up tidily. Sparkling ear pendants of a prodigious length hung from her dainty ears.

She looked, for all intents and purposes, as if she were about to jaunt off to one of her famous garden parties, flitting between her guests like a honeybee sampling the sweet nectar of the spring flowers. Only it was five o'clock in the morning. And she was smiling. *Smiling!*

Henree was sure she had gone completely mad. Summoned, he now stood uncertainly in the doorway to her bedchamber. It took him a moment or two to realize the sound he was hearing was laughter. She placed the single eyeglass she wore, suspended from a long golden chain around her neck, to her eye. She arched a delicate brow.

"Why Henree, you *do* look uncomfortable. Whatever is the matter?"

"Madame, I…nothing is the matter."

For a woman just turned sixty, Josephine was still quite handsome. Henree had been her steward for thirty years, so he knew her quite well and had always admired her beauty from a distance. It was a cold, stern sort of beauty that had always intrigued him. Her late husband had never appreciated it.

"Shall I wear my white scarf with the embroidered flowers, or the green one?"

"The white," Henree replied. "White looks lovely on your flawless skin."

"You have impeccable taste. Now I want you to relax."

Henree started to perspire. He hoped she wouldn't notice.

"I want you to tell me what the servants are saying about me."

"Madame?"

"Come now, Henree. How long have you known me?"

"Thirty years this Christmas, madame."

Josephine sighed.

"Thirty years, Henree. And in all that time, I've been a heartless, thoughtless bitch."

Henree nearly gasped. "Madame, certainly you have not…"

"Bah, Henree. Don't deny it. For thirty years, everything in this house has had to be just so. I've had to be the perfect hostess, the stodgy and dignified Josephine Huxley. I've demanded perfection from myself and those around me. I was so concerned with manners, with what others thought of me, with trying to impress my father— who wasn't happy about my marriage and never thought I'd amount to anything. Well, I tell you, I am not that woman anymore.

"So tell me. What are the servants saying?"

Henree fidgeted. "They are saying…they are saying you are not yourself."

Josephine sighed and rolled her wide green eyes heavenward. "You can do better than that, Henree. There's twenty dollars in it for you."

Now Henree was positively convinced the woman had gone silly. She counted every coin and spared no extra, unless she was acquiring the newest evening gowns trimmed with satin rouleaux, corkscrew gauze, or frills of blonde lace to impress her well-to-do guests. She had always had an eye for fashion.

"Loosen up old chap, or I'll find a new steward."

Henree's jaw dropped.

"That was a joke, Henree. You have served me faithfully and well, and I fully intend to make up for my years of stinginess. Now tell me what they are saying."

Henree cleared his throat.

"They are saying you should have…should have fallen on your arse a long time ago."

Josephine laughed so hard that tears threatened to spill down her ruddy cheeks.

71

"I should thank that old, crotchety horse," she remarked, "for dumping me on my backside. Henree, I saw my whole life flash before my eyes." She looked away for a moment, tiredness having leapt into her eyes. "And it was empty. *Empty*."

Josephine had always been an avid horsewoman. The fact that she had fallen off a horse one week ago had been a shock to everyone, but not nearly as shocking as her subsequent behavior.

Fortunately, she had only suffered bruises, for the rains had made the ground soft. She'd landed in a huge puddle, a tangled mess of velvet and mud.

Josephine let the eyeglass drop softly against her chest.

"Where are my white gloves?" she asked absently.

"Madame, you do realize the time?"

"I am not mad. Of course I realize the time. It's just that I can't afford to lose another minute. I've just had the most exciting news." She took a deep breath and the corners of her gracefully sculpted mouth lifted again, the smile returning to her eyes.

"I have a granddaughter." It bubbled out of her.

"A…granddaughter?" Henree asked.

Josephine's own daughter had died in her early twenties. She rarely talked about her. Henree wasn't sure why.

"I hired someone last week, after my...fall...to look into matters. You see, I did not approve of my daughter's choice of a husband. I wanted her to marry Simon Wethersby, but she would have none of it. I thought he was the most suitable choice. Ha! He's nearly in debtor's prison now. Has a brood of nine and can barely feed them. Shows you what I know about character. Not a thing!"

Josephine's eyes misted.

"I treated her like my father had treated me. Alexandra...ran off when she was eighteen. So young. I never saw her again. I pretended I never even had a daughter. It was cruel of me. I felt she owed me something since I had sacrificed so much to make her into a dignified, proud, educated woman. But what did I sacrifice?

"I didn't realize I was squelching her spirit, for she was very much like me. Determined. Stubborn. I pushed my pain aside and went on with my life. I was very proud. Too proud. I should have been there for her. I had no idea she was carrying a child then." Josephine's shoulders slumped slightly, uncharacteristically.

"I should have forgiven her. But I didn't understand. She was in love. I had never been in love. Still haven't been to this day. Lord, but we didn't marry for love."

"Madame, you are too hard on yourself. You always have been."

Josephine looked at Henree as if she were seeing him for the first time, the tall elegance of the man, the strength and loyalty of his spirit, the hard, sculpted muscles beneath his shirt. She quickly looked away.

"Everything had to be just so, just so, or I was sure I would be positively ruined if it was not. I did not talk of my daughter's...indiscretion. Summers passed and I began to search for her. Nobody knew anything." Josephine dabbed at her tears with a linen handkerchief.

"Oh madame, I am so sorry...."

Josephine put up her hand. "It's all my fault. Yes, I finally found out what I wanted to know, after all this time. And then to discover she was dead. I can't talk about that right now, but with bad news came good. She had a daughter, and she put her in an orphanage.

That much I know. My granddaughter is eighteen now, if she is alive and well. I hope and pray that she is, and that I will find her."

"Congratulations, madame," Henree said, smiling. "You'll make the perfect grandmother."

"Oh, I hope not, Henree. I hope I will be interfering, meddling, and overbearing. I hope I will be doting, give unwanted advice often, and make her throw her arms up in loving disgust. Anything but perfect. I've had about damn enough of perfect."

Henree nodded his elegant silver head in understanding, not used to hearing swear words coming from Josephine's lips.

Josephine retrieved her gloves from a drawer lined with linen and scented with jasmine, snapping them on crisply. She placed the white silken hat ornamented with flowers atop her head.

"I need an escort into town to talk with the detective. Are you coming?"

Henree grinned. "Absolutely, madame."

"I don't know her name, or where she lives, or anything at all! But I know Mr. Spencer will find out everything I need to know."

"And then what will you do, madame?"

Josephine took one more look at her reflection in the long, oaken dressing mirror, adjusting her hat to just the right angle. Then she turned a devilish smile on Henree.

"Why, spoil her rotten, of course. That's what grandmothers do, you know." She headed into the hallway, Henree trailing behind. "I just hope I'm not too late."

9

Lighted candles flickered softly on the mantle above the scalloped aqua hearth, and Genevieve, Harold, and Martha waited expectantly. Penley kept glancing at his pocket watch; Harold held a Bible on his lap.

"If I didn't know better, I'd say someone was getting married tonight," Camille said, her voice rising unsteadily. Dear God, she was even wearing white. She felt her knees go weak. She was greeted by looks of surprise. There was no sense in hanging on to her tavern speech now, for she wasn't going to fool anybody anymore. There was no reason to. And it was quite obvious that the guests had been informed of her decision by Nicholas.

"Camille will explain later," was all Nicholas said to the curious looks.

Genevieve was the first to congratulate her. "I knew you would accept my brother's proposal." She hugged Camille fiercely. "He can be very persuasive, you know."

Proposal? There had been no proposal...only the threat of physical violence if she didn't comply! But of course, Genevieve couldn't know about that. Could she?

Genevieve leaned closer, whispering so that only Camille could hear. "My God, but you are unexpected. You are exactly what my brother needs. I knew there was something about you...something I couldn't quite put my finger on."

What about my needs? Camille thought. She was in a state of shock. She was getting married. Tonight. Now. The next few moments were a blur. She balled her hands into fists at her sides, her stomach a tight knot. She concentrated on the pictures of Branton ancestors hanging above the fireplace. The dark, winged brows, the stern glances, the eyes which looked down on her with haughty disdain. She felt herself begin to sway and closed her eyes. Nicholas' hand was firm upon her arm. "Open your eyes, my sweet. I wouldn't want you to miss anything." He didn't attempt to hide the anger in his voice. The muscles in his jaw were taut and there was something cruel about his mouth.

The vows she and Nicholas spoke barely registered in her mind. Martha dabbed a hanky at her eyes, sniffling loudly and sighing about how romantic it was. Nicholas slipped a shiny, gold band from the pinky finger of his left hand and placed it on her finger. They were pronounced husband and wife shortly before midnight. The brief touch of his lips to hers broke the trance, the merest shiver of unexpected warmth from the hardness of his mouth.

Soon after, with much revelry, they were escorted upstairs, to the doorway of his room. Without warning, he swept her up, the backs of her knees pressed intimately against his arm. "Tradition has it I must carry you over the threshold, Mrs. Branton." He shouldered the door open and closed it with a booted foot.

"Put me down!" she cried.

"As you wish." He complied, taking his sweet time about it, letting her slide down the hard length of him. She quickly put distance between them.

"You're quite sure of yourself, aren't you?" she demanded.

"Consider it a character flaw. I have many."

"What if I'd said no? You had the ring on your finger. You had the preacher to dinner. Everyone seemed to know I was getting married tonight but me! And I came here to *avoid* marriage."

"There wasn't the slightest possibility you'd say no. I wouldn't have allowed it. It was going to happen sooner or later. I had to honor my word to my father and now I have. My obligation is fulfilled. From this moment on, we will remain strangers." His eyes traveled leisurely over her body, then came back to rest on her face. They burned like the golden glow of a candle at midnight. "Come now, my sweet, tell your new bridegroom how much you love him."

"You are the most arrogant and impossible man!" Camille said striding angrily through the door connecting their rooms. She had no idea where she was going; any door would do if it led away from him!

She had to turn around to close the door and her mouth dropped as he began removing his shirt. "By the way, that is your room. Goodnight, *Mrs.* Branton. Pleasant dreams, my sweet."

His deep, masculine voice slid gratingly over her fragile nerves. For the second time that evening, Camille felt an overwhelming desire to hurl something at his arrogant backside—something more solid than peas. And she wished she hadn't seen that broad expanse of chest, of hard muscle and soft, curling black hair, just before she slammed the door closed.

His physique—the corded muscles, the narrow waist, the powerful shoulders—bespoke of hard, physical work. Yet his hands were not callused. The man was an enigma.

A high-necked white cotton nightgown had been laid out on the bed. She stared at it for a moment, then changed out of her clothes and slipped it on, feeling as if she'd slid into the skin of another woman. This wasn't happening to her. This wasn't her life...couldn't be her life.

She blew out the candle on the stand next to the bed and lay in the darkness, listening to Nicholas' movements in the next room.

She heard him pacing, then the sound of his boots dropping to the floor. Did he sleep with nothing on? She pulled the covers tighter about her chin.

Then she thought of Christopher and her friend Meagan and she could not stop the flow of tears. She pressed her face into the pillow, crying as quietly as she could until she could cry no more. Hours later, when it was quiet, her heart stopped hammering and she fell into a fitful sleep.

10

Camille was awakened the next morning by the rustling of a servant stoking the fire in the hearth. She had been so angry last evening she hadn't bothered to take note of her surroundings. The room was done in muted green-gold tones and contained dainty Maplewood furniture. It looked like it hadn't been occupied in a long time.

"I hope I didn't disturb you miss," the servant said. "There are a few things in the armoire that you can make use of."

Camille peered groggily at the young girl. "What's your name?"

"Molly," she said smiling shyly as if she weren't used to anyone wanting to know her name.

"Thank you, Molly. You can call me Camille. What time is it?"

"I believe it's close to 10 o'clock, miss."

"Oh, it's late!" Camille exclaimed.

"Breakfast is still being served in the dining room. Would you like help dressing, miss?"

"No, thank you, Molly." She'd been dressing herself for years…why would she need a servant for that?

Molly nodded her head and left. Camille thumbed through the clothes hanging in the wardrobe and chose a simple green calico dress. There were shoes as well—she chose a simple pair of matching green slippers that were a trifle big on her feet, but not so large that she couldn't manage.

She made her way to the dining room, and as she approached it, she heard Genevieve's warm laughter mingled with a child's. She was relieved to note that Nicholas was not present.

"Good morning Camille, I trust you slept well," she said, a trace of concern in her eyes. Camille blushed as she realized what everyone would be thinking—that the marriage had been consummated, that Nicholas had taken her to his bed. Apparently, their agreement that the marriage be in name only was between the two of them.

"As well as can be expected," Camille said.

"I'd like you to meet Arabelle and Damaris," Genevieve said.

"Wait!" one of the girls cried. "We're twins. She has to guess who's who!"

The ten-year-old girls looked remarkably alike. The one who had spoken had large brown eyes and chestnut-hair threaded with pink ribbon. There was definitely a look of Nicholas about her; her face with its dark brows and impish smile was completely charming.

The other girl turned away from Camille as if disinterested. "We're getting too old for these silly games," she said coolly. Her hair was a shade darker, her set eyes a bit deeper in her face. There was something dour about her countenance, and she wore no ribbons in her hair. Camille imagined she could be very pretty if she smiled.

"Well, let's see," Camille replied. She looked at the girl with the pink ribbons, who spooned a forkful of fried eggs into her mouth.

"You must be Arabelle," she said, "and you must be Damaris."

Arabelle squealed with delight. "How did you know?" she asked.

"It was a lucky guess, nothing more," Damaris said darkly. Camille was amazed that two people could look so alike yet appear to have such different personalities.

Damaris eyed Camille curiously. A twisted smile spread across her face and there was something almost cruel about it. "You're the lady who fell in the river," she said. Camille was about to retort that she hadn't *fallen* into the river, then thought that it wouldn't be right to paint such a callous picture of their father. "And you're wearing one of my mama's dresses."

Camille felt a twitter of unease. The clothes hanging in the wardrobe...had they belonged to Marlena?

"But she didn't drown like mama," Arabelle added.

Damaris looked sharply at Arabelle. "She didn't drown, Arabelle. If she'd drown, they'd have found her body. And they never did, did they?

"I've heard the servants talk, haven't you? They always think we're not listening because we're children; that we can't understand what they're saying. They say grandfather made her go away because she was a bad woman. They say daddy wanted her dead. One day she disappeared and she never came back...."

Genevieve eyed Damaris sternly. "That kind of talk is inappropriate," she said. "The servants should not be whispering among themselves. And you shouldn't listen to such talk." Damaris just shrugged her shoulders.

"Arabelle, did you know Camille is our new mother? She married daddy last night."

Arabelle grinned broadly. "Is it really true? That would be wonderful!"

"It is true, Arabelle," Genevieve said, "but now you are both late for your lessons and Mr. Potter won't like that one bit, now will he? There will be plenty of time to get acquainted later. Now run along."

Arabelle happily complied. Damaris lingered for a moment. "Arabelle is...naïve," she said, struggling with the word. "But I'm not. I don't *want* a new mother. Maybe daddy will send you away too."

She left the room and Genevieve apologized for her behavior. "You see, Camille, the…tragedy…affected her more deeply than Arabelle. Arabelle is a sunny-natured child and Damaris, well Damaris takes some getting used to."

Though she longed to know more about what happened to Nicholas' first wife, she didn't want to pry. "I lost my parents when I was very young," she said and quickly changed the subject. "Will Nicholas be joining us?" she asked, hoping Genevieve didn't notice the catch in her voice.

Genevieve shook her head. "No, he's gone into the city on business and will not return until tomorrow."

"In that case, I thought I might return to the city today to collect my things." Camille desperately wanted to see Meagan, to make sure she was all right.

"I'll have the coach brought around after breakfast," Genevieve said. She laid her hand on Camille's shoulder. "I know you must feel a bit out of place right now, but everything will work out. You'll see. I'm sorry to leave you so soon, but I must check on one of the servants. She just had a baby and it was a difficult time." She smiled

and left Camille to eat breakfast while the coach was summoned.

Later, as the black-lacquered coach rambled toward the city,

Camille was suddenly struck with the thought that she was a *wife*,

and Dear God, expected to be a mother to his twin daughters.

Already Damaris resented her presence. She'd failed miserably in

her quest to avoid this marriage, and that wide-shouldered, black-

haired blue-blood was to blame. If he hadn't been so insistent on

honoring his father's dying wish…if she hadn't feared Meletios'

meaty fists so much…. Perhaps it would have been preferable to

suffer a beating. Camille shivered.

And Dear God, what about Christopher? There had been no time

to write to him, to plead with him to come and put a stop to the

marriage. Perhaps if she wrote to him as soon as she could, begged

him to come for her, Nicholas wouldn't care. He'd said it would be a

marriage in name only. As long as she was discreet, they could meet

and...and do whatever it was that lovers did in secret. The thought

gave her hope. It was the only promise of love she'd ever had, and

she was going to hold onto it.

11

Nicholas sat staring out the second story window of his shipping offices. The streets below were gutted with carriages and people hurrying about in the muddied streets. Try as he might, he could not concentrate on the tasks at hand and that was due to the green-eyed vixen he'd married last night.

The truth was, for the better part of the day, he'd been putting off a most unpleasant task—speaking to the girl's uncle. He wanted to know more about Penley's relationship with his father, wanted to make a few things clear to the man as well.

It was growing toward dusk and he wanted to get that over with then spend a night lavishly satisfying his passions with his mistress.

He may be a married man now, but it was in name only and he had no plans to deny himself his pleasures.

Slinging his jacket over a shoulder, he headed downstairs, determined to find out more about Camille and the arrangement his father had made with her uncle.

The slight breeze coming off the water stroked his dark hair as he walked along the crowded streets toward The Black Garter, lost in his own thoughts. His head came up sharply when he noticed the coach with the Branton family emblem blazed on the sides.

"Damn me!" he said, picking up his pace.

12

There was nothing special about the bawdy river house—it was a far cry from the fashionable cabarets and bordellos, the ballrooms, theaters, and cafes of the Vieux Carre, but at least it was not sunk so low as those establishments above Canal Street.

It was a two-story shack with a low gabled roof, built of rough cypress planks from old flatboats. Mostly it was the local riff raff who came in, just as they were, looking for a hot, greasy meal, a cold spurt of ale, and a good game of cards.

It was a favorite resort of river men, thieves, footpads, firebugs, even pirates. Occasionally the more legitimate citizens of the town would wander in by mistake. Mother Stephens, a waddling old harridan, had run the place for years.

The room that opened onto the street was the bar, and behind that was a large chamber with tables set up for gambling. One corner of the room was partitioned off by thin boards and served as a kitchen, dining room, and sleeping quarters; another corner was divided by curtains into smaller rooms where guests, upon payment of a picayune, might repair with women of the evening.

Outside, a church overlooked the water. There was an old abbey where one could still see the occasional gaunt figure clad in a loose habit of coarse, brown cloth with a hempen girdle about his waist and wooden sandals on his feet.

There was also a watch house, a prison, a hospital, and an arsenal. Then there were the beautiful three-story brick homes with their tiled roofs and courtyards and patios and narrow gardens with latticework. Now, after the events of the last twenty-four hours, it all seemed different to Camille. She didn't belong here; she didn't belong in Nicholas' world.

She pushed aside the curtain and gasped at the sight that greeted her. "Meagan, my God!" Meagan lay in the bed, the right side of her face puffy and blue, her right eye swollen shut.

Camille kneeled by the side of the bed and stroked Meagan's hair. "You should've told him everything, Meg. You shouldn't have held out. My God, I never thought he would resort to this."

A tear slid down Meagan's face. "Oh, but it hurts even to cry. I'm so sorry."

Camille frowned. "I'm going to help you. I'll explain everything later, but I have some money now." She put it in Meagan's fist. "I'm sending for a doctor. And just let Mother Stephens try and stop me. There'll be enough left over for you to get away from this place eventually."

"But…" Meagan began.

"I can't stay now. I have to go. I'll send someone to check on you. Get some rest now. And don't worry about Mother Stephens. I'll take care of that too."

Meagan nodded her head. Camille gently squeezed Meg's hand. "I'll come back. I promise."

Quietly, Camille drew the curtain shut and made for the door. She didn't want to be seen.

"Hey lassie, me cup runneth dry!" yelled a beastly, rotund man with a red, splotchy face and teeth that could have belonged to a horse. His portly, monstrous arm reached out and snaked around her small waist, pulling her down onto his lap.

"Don't ye look pretty today, lass. Pretty enough to kiss!" Camille stopped squirming when she realized it was exciting the grotesque man and only served to spur on the loud guffaws coming from around the table.

"I don't work here no more," she said, adopting her tavern speech.

"Aye, the little vixen is an uppity wench now. Don't work here no more! I've had me eye on you, girl. Ye may not be servin' tables today, but ye'll be servin' me manly needs soon enough!" He shoved an empty tankard into her hand. "Now be a good little gal and get me another drink first, will ye?"

Camille was alarmed. "Let me go; I said I don't work here no more." She gave him a smile that would have melted gold, but still he did not release her.

"Yer the prettiest thing I seed in years, wench, and I don't think I'll let ya go without yer givin' me a big kiss," he snarled. "And what's with them fancy rags you got on?"

Camille's mind raced in revulsion. She said a silent prayer to God asking him to let the chortling bear of a man release her! Amazingly, the slug's arm slackened a bit and the smile disappeared from his big, meaty face. She followed his gaze across the room to the tall figure eclipsing the doorway and gasped. He looked furious. His dark eyes flashed daggers as they surveyed the room. She heard the whispers around her.

"Ain't that a Branton?"

Very funny, God! If there was one thing she feared even more than a lusty patron, it was Nicholas Branton.

She had never seen him looking so angry. What was he doing here? Sweet Lord, if she hadn't gotten herself into a fine mess this time! Yet she couldn't take her eyes off him.

He towered over the other men in the room and commanded the center of attention.

His black hair glistened in the flickering candlelight. As he got closer, Camille could see the hard set of his jaw, the graze of dark whiskers on his chin, the menacing look in his dark eyes. His tight black breeches outlined the powerful build of his thighs, and the sleeves of his white shirt were rolled back, revealing sleekly muscled forearms.

No doubt he was rankled about the inconvenience their little arrangement was causing him. He cornered Mother Stephens, who despite her considerable girth, seemed to shrink away from him. "I'm looking for my wife, Camille. You're going to tell me where she is."

"Yer *wife?*" she said, looking puzzled. "You must be mistaken...."

"Yes, my wife. We were married last night," he said. "Now you're going to stop wasting my time and tell me where she is. She's leaving with me and she's never setting foot in this establishment again."

The fat, cowering woman pointed a grubby finger in Camille's direction.

"You'll find her o'er there Sir, but mind ye, I have no one to fill her shift...." Her voice trailed off at the incredulous look that sprung into his eyes.

Nicholas clenched his fists and slowly turned a heated gaze in Camille's direction. There was nowhere left to hide. That corner of the room cleared out quickly, patrons overturning wobbly, uneven tables and spilling ale in their wake. Slowly, his thickly muscled legs covered the distance between them.

"If you know what's good for you, you'll take your hands off my wife," Nicholas growled.

"Is that so, ye bleedin' sod? This pretty little thing, who was about to spread 'er legs for me, is yer wife?"

Camille struggled in his arms, noting the gold storm in Nick's eyes. A slow, malicious smile crept over his face.

The red-bearded man stood up and released her, ready for a fight. Camille backed away, until her small form pressed against the back wall, her heart beating wildly.

The sailor reached down and pulled a jagged knife from his boot, smiling lecherously. "What ye gonna do now, sod?"

"That depends mate," Nicholas said. His eyes were intense, blazing with bronze sparks. Camille had seen him angry before, but never like this.

The man threw his head back and laughed, then suddenly charged Nicholas. Nicholas caught his beefy arm in a deathly grip and twisted it, knocking the knife to the floor. The sailor was built like a tree trunk and the two men struggled. Nicholas got the upper hand and his fist connected with the man's chin, causing him to stagger back.

He charged Nicholas again, and this time, the pair tumbled over a table onto the floor. Both stood up quickly, circling each other.

"Nicholas!" Camille shouted.

Nicholas turned just as one of the sailor's mates swung a chair at his head. He ducked, the rough edges of the chair leg grazing his cheek, and repositioned himself.

"You want some too?" Nicholas said. "Happy to oblige." With a few quick movements, a few strong jabs, the man lay in a heap on the floor. Growing impatient, Nicholas pulled a pistol from the back of his trousers and brought it close to the red-bearded man's face.

"You ain't gonna use that, mate," he said, hesitantly. "She ain't worth *that* much trouble." He raised his hands in defeat and took a step backward.

"You're right," Nicholas said, his other fist shooting out, breaking jawbone and knocking the big man unconscious. "I'm not going to use it."

He tucked the pistol neatly into the back of his trousers, his eyes locking with Camille's. He closed the distance between them quickly.

"I find you here, after I expressly forbade it?" His eyes traveled over her appearance and he frowned as they lingered on the creamy mounds of flesh straining at the low-cut bodice of her green dress.

He reached out a finger to touch a lock of her honey-colored hair, then pulled on it, bringing her face mere inches from his, his other hand tangling in her soft hair. His voice was strained.

"No wife of a Branton goes waltzing off as she pleases to work in a filthy tavern for a pittance. Do you understand?"

His eyes challenged hers to respond, to say even one word. Dear God, he thought she was *working*? Suddenly she remembered the tankard thrust into her hand. The rough sailors' lies about what she was going to do for him. "I wasn't...."

"God knows what else you've been doing under this roof, but as long as you're my wife, that stops too."

Camille was incensed. Her green eyes flashed emerald fire.

"Release me at once, sir. I am neither your property nor your slave. If you wish to talk to me as a civilized human being, we'll finish this discussion outside." She set the tankard on a nearby table.

Nicholas released her in disbelief and watched as she held her head high and sashayed out of the establishment, every male eye in the place following her.

Nicholas shivered unexpectedly at the thought of what could have befallen her if he hadn't showed up when he had, but the fear was suddenly replaced by anger. The thought that she had been giving other men what he, her lawfully wedded husband, had not demanded, suddenly made him furious. He was right behind her, the two of them all but tumbling into the black coach waiting outside.

13

As she settled herself on the velvet-covered seat, squeezing her small form into the corner, Camille wished she had a horse, one that would carry her far away from Nicholas. She was already tired of the ornate carriage with its heavy leather door that carried the bold Branton family crest, the tiny little cushions that matched the maroon trimmings of the carriage.

Camille would not meet Nicholas' eyes. "I have never been talked to in such a degrading manner, sir, and I find your insolence highly detestable," she said.

"You would play the lady now? I would not expect your patrons to be quoting Shakespeare or singing you love ballads. And call me

Nicholas. You're my wife, for God's sake, even if it's in name only." He raked his hand through his hair. "I didn't agree to this marriage so you could saunter about and besmirch my family's name. We haven't been married but a day and you don't have the decency to honor our agreement?" His eyes narrowed dangerously. "If I'd known you were a whore, I would never have agreed to the marriage."

Camille felt as if she'd been slapped in the face. First he had thought her a thief. Now he thought her a whore? Just what did he think she was doing at the tavern? A deeper flush crept up her neck and cheeks at the horrid thought, and she couldn't find her tongue. A great lump was forming in her throat and she felt as if she were choking. He grabbed her hand. The jolted touch was like fire, alarming and mesmerizing at the same time.

"The ring on your finger means you belong to me. We had an agreement. You're the wife of a Branton. You will come to understand what that means and not to question my authority."

She nearly laughed in his face, only she didn't feel in the least like laughing. It seemed, in the short time since they'd met, Nicholas always thought the worst of her.

"I should think, with the vast Branton fortunes at your disposal, you should not need to serve drunks in a wenching establishment."

Camille turned away from his probing eyes to stare out at the fading city and the darkness. The moon cast a silver-yellow glow over the countryside. She was trying desperately to keep her upper lip from trembling, to keep the tears from spilling down her cheeks.

Everything—the events of the past few days tumbling one upon the other, his accusations, the threat of being beaten by Meletios, what Meletios had done to Meagan, the unplanned wedding ceremony—it was all too much. But she would not correct his misimpressions. She didn't care what he thought.

The pair was silent; each lost in their own thoughts. After a while, she turned to him.

"Is this what brought you out, to tell me you have a reputation to uphold and that I may have some of your charity if I need it?"

If there was one thing Camille had learned in the past few years, it was that the steps of charity were steep indeed. "I will only say this once. You do not know me at all. I think we have made a grave mistake," she continued. "I don't want your charity. I want nothing from you."

"Do you have any idea what could have happened to you?" Nicholas asked, as if he hadn't heard her.

"I can take care of myself," Camille said. "I've worked in the tavern a long time."

"Can you? That's not what I witnessed tonight. What if that man took his knife and plunged it into you after he was through spreading your legs? Look at me, Camille."

When she wouldn't, Nicholas reached over and pulled her onto his lap. His rough fingers cupped her chin, forcing her to look into his eyes. Her bottom was nestled in the hard cradle of his thighs, a much too intimate position.

"Perhaps I had you figured wrong. Do you like the rough sort, Camille? I bet you know how to drive a man to distraction." His voice was low now, seeming to scrape at the constrained darkness of the carriage.

"I don't..." Camille said but was silenced by the touch of his lips upon hers, hard, eager, angry. She tried to push him away but his lips were firm, demanding, his breath hot and sweet with the lingering taste of brandy.

His lips searched hers, tasting, teasing, taunting. Despite her best efforts to resist, a shock of warmth flooded her soul. His hard male form was pressed tightly against her, yet his lips were soft and caressing, almost possessive. She found herself wanting to taste him, her body traitorously hungry for some small measure of warmth. His long, lean fingers threaded through her silky, golden hair, scattering pins in their wake.

His lips continued down her throat, weaving a hot trail until they returned to plunder her mouth again, his tongue forcing her lips open to his rough exploration. Camille heard him groan and then, just as suddenly, he released her.

"As I expected," he said, "you are no innocent." Camille felt the moment evaporate like the morning mist, and was rendered speechless once more.

"We are alone now. How could you stop me from taking what is rightfully mine, what now belongs to no other man? I am certain you would prefer my lovemaking to that beast of a man who had you on his lap."

Camille trembled. "You...you said you would not demand your husbandly rights."

His eyes, a mixture of gold heat and ice, skirted her form. "Do not fear. I am not as callous and cruel as you may think. I do not possess the same sort of morals as one of your tavern patrons. Besides, you are not the type of woman I normally desire."

It was then that she noticed the bruise and scrape on his left cheek. Instinctively she reached to touch it. "You're hurt," she said quietly.

He jerked at her touch, grabbing her hand quickly and moving it aside. "It's nothing."

Sternly, he set her away from him and they sat the rest of the trip in silence.

14

Nicholas did not look at her. His thoughts disturbed him. Still, the way she had responded to him puzzled him; there was innocence to her silky, heated kisses and yet a passion that promised so much more. And despite what she was, who she was, he couldn't deny that he wanted her badly…wanted to rip open her bodice and expose her soft, rounded breasts to the roughness of his hands.

He found himself wishing he were the first to show her the pleasures that could be had between a man and a woman. He had to stop thinking such thoughts or he might end up breaking his promise never to touch her—a promise that was now causing him physical pain for his manhood was swollen beneath the cloth of his trousers.

Belatedly, he thought of his mistress Lavinia and realized his night of passion would have to wait.

In the darkness he stared at Camille's soft profile, the outline of her lush lips, noted the rise and fall of her breasts beneath her flimsy garment as she breathed. She wasn't a virgin. Perhaps he would take what he wanted, when she was ready. For despite her heated words, she *had* responded to him. There was no denying that.

15

Camille felt dazed and confused by what had happened. Unknowingly, she traced her lips, lips that were slightly swollen from his kisses, with her trembling fingertips. The carriage was stifling, the night air unusually oppressive and humid, and she longed for the comfort of her room—the room she had so graciously been granted as hers and hers alone, though a door connected her room with his.

It was taking a sobering long time to get home! The streets were choked with water from the recent rains and the soil was slippery. In the balmy winds, oil lamps nailed to wooden posts swung haphazardly from their projecting arms.

Obviously, Nicholas was toying with her. He was an arrogant man, a wealthy man, an experienced man who had probably had many lovers. Her embarrassment abated and was replaced by relief at the thought that he really had no desire for her; he was just exposing her to further humiliation. After all, he'd said she wasn't his type.

Genevieve had said she was just what Nicholas needed. Why had she had such a thought, when they were so clearly wrong for each other? Camille felt a strange ache in her heart. She was sure she wasn't Nicholas Branton's type. She was sure no gentleman would ever want her, would ever have proposed marriage to her in the way she had dreamed about since she was a little girl. There was no sense in conjuring up that dream ever again.

She could imagine the sophisticated, beautiful ladies Nicholas had charmed into his bed. She'd only been kissed once before, and hadn't found the experience pleasurable. It didn't sit well with her that she'd discovered it could be pleasurable, and that Nicholas Branton was the one to show her. Well, it wouldn't happen again. She didn't need any lessons from him.

They finally arrived at the mansion, the carriage passing down the long, wooded lane. Pinewood and the hot, sharp scent of magnolia blooms lingered on the night air.

As she alighted from the carriage, ignoring the hand he offered to her, she didn't dare look into those heated gold-brown eyes. She was caught in a world she barely remembered as a child, a world where she didn't belong. Her husband thought her a thief and a common whore. Her uncle had successfully ridded himself of her. She had no family to speak of and precious few friends.

She raced up the hulking porch stairs, ghostly white magnolia petals waving behind her in the breeze. She waltzed through the foyer and hurriedly climbed the marble staircase, retiring to her quarters—and he to his.

Both doors slammed, one after the other.

16

Kipp Gresham stood in Nicholas' study idling twirling the chain of his gold pocket watch around his finger. His light blue eyes looked both amused and concerned. "You look terrible, old chap. Like you slept in your clothes."

Kipp was one of the few men Nicholas had befriended over the years, one of the few men he trusted. They'd spent a considerable amount of years carousing, gaming, and pursuing some of the *ton's* most notable and 'unattainable' ladies in London—unattainable, that is, until they'd set about seducing them into their respective beds. Because of their obligations and travels, they hadn't seen each other in nearly a year.

"You look different. Almost like a married man the day after his wedding. I've seen you look like that once before...."

Nicholas grunted. "You know damn well too much about me...and always before I get the chance to tell you myself. Don't tell me it's already made the gossip columns."

"Why, yes, old chap, it has. Imagine it. There I was, sitting down to my first breakfast back in the states. I was reading the newspaper and the most alarming paragraph slaps me in the face!" Kipp pulled the article out of his pocket and gave it to Nicholas. He began to read:

It is strongly rumored that Nicholas Branton, son of international shipping magnate Caindale Branton, wed shortly after his father's recent death to a woman of unknown pedigree. This is a rather shocking development, as it is well known to the community that Nicholas' first wife is presumed to have drowned, her body was never recovered. It was also assumed the notable rake would never marry again. It is known that the younger Mr. Branton's first marriage was not a happy union. Why did he bet on marriage again? Let's

hope this one goes more smoothly for him and his new lady.

Nicholas looked up when he was done reading. "Since when do you read gossip columns?"

Kipp ignored the question. "A rather grave loss for ladies the world over, I thought."

"It's true. I am married. I was hoodwinked by my own father, from the grave. I was married several nights ago."

Kipp laughed. "I can't wait to meet the little filly who managed to corral you. Lavinia will be so disappointed."

Nicholas frowned. "Actually, my dear chap, I had to marry her. It was a provision of my father's will. A deathbed request. Well, not really a request. In order to inherit his properties and wealth, I had to agree to the match. However, it turned out to be a rather profitable business transaction. I've inherited my father's properties as well as his ships, so I've had the last laugh. I've been running his business for the past five years anyway; I'm the one who built it back up after Philip left." He frowned.

117

"If Philip reads about Caindale's death, wherever he is, and comes back expecting to be Lord of the manor, he's in for a rude surprise."

Nicholas filled Kipp in on all the details—the urchin's attempt to have the arrangement called off, her former occupation at the tavern, her uncle's bold threats, and the unexpected provisions of his father's will. He told Kipp he and his wife had come to a mutual agreement—the marriage would be in name only—but only they, and now Kipp too, knew that.

"It doesn't make any sense," Kipp said, pouring himself a brandy. "Why would your father subject you to that? Did he know the girl?"

"My father never missed an opportunity to ridicule me. First, it was neglect. Then when I started to demonstrate my business acumen, and when Philip humiliated him with his own disappearing act, it turned to ridicule *and* revenge. I have my suspicions about how my father knew her and her uncle, and I'm sure it was his final chance to humiliate me by forcing the marriage to the little whore.

Caindale probably owed the man a huge gambling debt and he wanted her off his hands."

"That's a bit harsh, isn't it?"

Nicholas frowned, grabbed a bottle of bourbon and poured himself a liberal drink. "It's true. She's … experienced, if you prefer those terms. And if Philip wasn't going to inherit, I was my father's last choice. Of course I should have known there would be stipulations."

Nicholas raked a hand irritably through his hair. "She's not my type, but she is attractive. She's also very good at projecting an aura of innocence—at playing the virgin, which she quite clearly is not. You'll meet her soon enough."

"I'm looking forward to it. You could always hire an investigator, you know. To find Philip." Kipp noted the anger, the gold, glacial glint of his friend's eyes, his fists as he clenched the newspaper article in one hand and the glass of bourbon in the other.

"She's had quite an effect on you. What you need, my friend, is a good night of gaming and fighting. What do you say?"

"Make it a night of wenching and you're on."

Kipp arched a sandy brow and smiled. "The ladies will be quite relieved that marriage has not changed your rakish ways, Nick." Kipp poured himself a glass of brandy. "Cheers, old fellow. I see no reason why we can't get an early start on the evening."

17

There was another man who was quite intrigued by the newspaper article. He'd almost missed the small paragraph as he scanned the forwarded newspaper, now a week old. He smiled to himself as he watched the trade clouds pile in tumbling heights to the north, their lower ridges scalloped with flame. The ocean sighed and stirred with unhurried speed until it reached the sandy shores.

"What are you thinking about, love?" The man turned his head and took in the vision of loveliness standing before him. She wore a tight-bodiced dress that molded her bosom in youthful maturity; her fiery auburn hair shimmered in the hot sunlight. Her grey eyes were curious, the eyes that had intrigued him from the moment he'd seen her. They were like the depths of the coldest November day—brilliant, shaded, and ashen against her hair.

"I was thinking of you, as I always am," she said. She began to massage his shoulders. He closed his eyes.

"It's time, my love." He thought of the opulent paradise where they'd both been living under false names, the leisurely, sun-drenched days, and the hot, sultry nights of lovemaking. In a way, he would be sorry to leave it. His adrenaline flowed. He opened his eyes and silently handed her the newspaper.

She scanned it, quickly finding the article. Her eyes grew wide.

"Our patience has been rewarded."

They sat down in the sand. "I can't believe old Caindale is dead. And I can't wait to see Nicholas' expression when you waltz back into his life," she breathed. She looked toward the sea and absently dug her bare toes into the silky sand. He forced her beneath him suddenly, his eyes growing lustful. "I hope you are not looking forward to it overly much, my dear." He remembered the first forbidden kiss he'd stolen from her, the way she had eagerly molded her body to his, the way the braid of his uniform had dug into his body as they lay pressed together, her husband only two rooms away.

She laughed wickedly. "Rot his soul. What I look forward to is his demise. "

"That's more like it, love." With savage fierceness, he hungrily took her. They lost all sense of time until the horizon became purple-domed. As the sky splintered into blue-black night and the stars glittered like sharply cut diamonds, he took her again. "This will be our last night here," he breathed. "We can't waste time. Tomorrow we set sail for the states."

His lips curled in agile glee. The last thing Nicholas Branton needed was another complication. "And he thought he was done with us, love. What a bitter surprise he'll have. A bitter surprise indeed!"

18

"I still can't believe he married *her*," the maid said, folding a linen napkin just so. The other maid continued polishing the silver to perfection.

"A common tavern maid, a lower station than a maid! And the rumor is she didn't *want* to marry him! Can you imagine! I heard she has the table manners of a boar and a spiked tongue to boot. None of it makes any sense. I can't believe he's going to present her to the world as his wife. She'll make a fool of herself!"

She looked at her reflection in the shiny spoon she was holding. She fluffed her dark hair with the other hand. "Why *I'm* a better catch."

"You girls need more to do?"

Both girls snapped to attention as Lucy sauntered into the dining room.

"You don't know nothin' 'bout the girl, so don't be so quick to judge her. We got lots to do before that party and no time for chit chat."

Both girls nodded their heads and resumed working in silence. For sure they would pick up their conversation later, and they looked forward to learning every sordid detail of the upcoming ball.

19

Genevieve sat in the drawing room, her glossy black hair and smooth complexion set off to distinction by the Italian blue dress she wore. "I'll pay you handsomely to teach her as much dancing, basic French, and etiquette as you can in the next three days," Genevieve said. "We don't have much time. The girls will be given a reprieve from their lessons. They are studying Latin, aren't they? So I'm sure they won't mind. Will you do it?"

"A most unusual situation," Romey Potter commented, scratching his chin with his finger. "I'll have to think about it."

"Of course you will be discreet," she added, fluttering her thick dark lashes. "It's best if Nicholas doesn't know about the arrangement. The grand ball is Friday. I've already had her to the dressmakers and forced her through several rushed fittings. I'm having several dresses made of different colors and fabrics, just in case she insists on turning down my charity. I want to tempt her with satins, laces, and velvets. There's got to be one dress that she can't resist. What woman wouldn't want a beautiful dress adorning her figure?" Genevieve rose and smiled sweetly. He didn't know it yet, but Romey Potter was already wrapped around her little finger. "Do we have a deal?"

Romey nodded. "But we don't know how this experiment is going to turn out, Miss Genevieve. From what you told me before, we have a lot of work to do. I don't know if I'll be successful."

Genevieve rolled her eyes, mumbling something about men and how stubborn they were, and left Romey to go teach his lessons and give the girls the good news. No Latin for three whole days. They would be tickled pink. And maybe for once, she'd see Damaris smile. It'd been so long since she'd seen her genuinely smile.

20

"I've never danced with a gentleman before," Camille

remarked. "In fact, I've never danced at all. I'll probably step all

over your toes."

"It doesn't matter," Romey said, laughing. "You don't have to

be an expert. You just have to listen to the music, feel it in your heart

and the rest will happen. You'll look like you know what you're

doing. Besides, not all those attending the party are considered

gentlemen."

They were walking down magnificent steps adorned with curled

wrought iron railings into the broad sweeping garden. Was it only

days ago that Camille had been lost in these very gardens, wondering what it would be like to be the lady of the house? And now she *was*

Mrs. Nicholas Branton. It was all so unreal.

At first Camille had been angry about the arrangement

Genevieve had made to 'tutor' her in the fine graces of being Mrs.

Branton. But then she'd realized Genevieve was probably the only

person trying to help her and had decided to humor her request. Plus,

her mood was lightened a little by the fact that a doctor had seen to

Meagan and she was on the mend.

Romey Potter was only an inch or so taller than she was and

very studious looking with his wire-rimmed glasses.

"I thought you might like some privacy until you feel

comfortable with the steps," Romey said, absently fiddling with his

glasses. "There's a secluded arbor not far from here. We can practice

there."

A faint breeze carrying the scent of verbenas slid over them.

Despite the warmth, Camille was comfortable. She wore her own

clothes, her best blouse and skirt. Though they were somewhat worn,

they were sturdy. After the incident in the tavern, Genevieve had

thought to send for her things, a small blessing, considering her own husband forbade her to go back to the tavern. And she was not about to put another one of Marlena's dresses on.

She studied the orange trees basking in the heat and the pink and mauve roses trailing the borders of the path. Eventually, they came to the arbor. "Mr. Potter, what about music?"

"Call me Romey. I'm glad you asked. We're not going to need music, Camille. It is alright if I call you Camille?" She nodded and he took her hand, leading her into the center of the arbor. Tall trees, thick bushes with budding pink flowers, and a circular hedge of boxwoods hemmed them in. "Now, I want you to close your eyes and think of your favorite song. Anything."

Camille closed her eyes. "Ok. I've thought of something, a song I love. But I don't know what it's called."

"That's alright. Just imagine yourself in an elegant ballroom; see the musicians sitting on the dais. The candles are flickering. The musicians raise their bows...."

Camille smiled. She'd never been to a ball, but she could imagine what it would be like. She didn't have the heart to tell Romey that his task was hopeless; they had less than three days to turn her into a lady of sophistication and grace. And what did it matter anyway? Nicholas would expect her to falter, to make grievous social missteps.

He would dance one dance with her for show, because he had to, and then he would probably leave her to her own devices. He would expect her to act the part of a loving wife in public, but would he act the part of devoted husband?

Camille felt a new determination. She would learn everything she could. She would match him move for move. She would be graceful and sophisticated; she would hold her head high. She would act like she belonged. She had promised to play the part, and she would. She just hoped he wouldn't be expecting her to play it so well.

"Just listen to the music and my voice. Concentrate while I tell you about etiquette," Romey said.

"Ladies are first to be cared for, to have the best seats, and are always entitled to courteous protection. Your husband will dance the first set with you but is not expected to dance with you otherwise. That would be unfair to the other guests.

Now a good dance partner neither leads nor follows but trusts and anticipates. Be careful how you refuse to dance with a gentleman; if you plead fatigue, do not dance with another. Dance quietly, do not caper about, and dance only from the hips downward. And always carry two pairs of gloves; if one pair gets soiled from handling refreshments, you can slip discreetly from the room, change to a fresh pair, and return with none the wiser. And if a gentlemen should pinch you...."

"If a gentleman should pinch me, he'll get a slap across the cheek," Camille said.

Romey looked concerned.

"I'm not serious, Romey." Camille thought of how often she'd been pinched at the tavern. She'd learned it was best to just ignore it.

Romey looked relieved. "We'll start with the waltz," he said, "which began as an Austrian peasant dance. It's very popular in Europe though some think it vulgar. It's quite beautiful, I think. But if you feel uncomfortable with any of the movements, just say so."

"I should be able to pick that one up," Camille said quietly. "After all, I'm just a peasant." *Somebody's stupid wench.* Her uncle's cruel words echoed in her mind.

Romey placed his finger under her chin and she opened her eyes. "You are only a peasant if you think you are. You have more natural grace and sincerity than most of the wealthy ladies I know, and I have faith in you. Now enough feeling sorry for yourself." He dropped his hands and began to demonstrate, pretending he had a partner.

"The basic steps of the waltz can be learned in a short time. The other dances require more practice. We're going to roll, turn, and glide in time with the music."

He took her hands and began to show her. "Step-step-close. Step-step-close."

"Oh!" Camille faltered, stepping on his foot again and again and again.

"We're not leaving here until you have it right."

"You are merciless, Romey. And your poor feet!"

He smiled. "My feet are fine. It's true they haven't taken a beating like this since I taught poor Mrs. Allister's daughter to dance, but it's worth it. Once you have this down, you can pretty much fake your way through the evening–even if you don't know the mazurka, the schottische, or the gallop."

An hour later, she had made considerable progress. "Now one more time, and then I think Miss Genevieve has plans for your afternoon."

By now, they had got the rhythm of the dance and waltzed easily around the arbor. Romey smiled proudly. "Your husband will be pleasantly surprised."

"I'd say so."

They started at the sound of the gruff voice.

"I hope you've saved a dance for me, wife."

His eyes were gold-bronze sparks touching her like late afternoon sunshine on a frozen lake. His arms were crossed casually over his chest as he leaned against the base of a tree watching them. How long had he been there?

He looked at Romey. "I'd like a moment with my wife."

Romey nodded and slunk away.

Nicholas strode toward Camille and stopped directly in front of her, leaving mere inches between them. He reached out and took a silken strand of her hair in his fingers. "Now that the tavern men are off limits, you are seducing the hired help?"

Camille pushed his hand away, smoothing the errant tendril back in place. Of course he would think the worst of her. Why did it surprise her each and every time he did it? It would never cross his mind that she might be taking a dancing lesson so that she would keep up her end of the bargain, look presentable to his guests at the party? After all, he'd had everything handed to him. He'd grown up in the lap of luxury; he knew all the rules. All the dances. Which fork to use first. He didn't even have to think about it. And even if he broke the rules, he was a man; he would be forgiven.

Camille poked his broad chest with her finger. "You're not the smoothest wheel on the cart, are you? You may be wealthy, but your manners are atrocious. You always seem to say what you think *before* you think about it." She continued poking him. "And you can think what you like," Camille said. "I don't care."

She turned to walk away but he gripped her arm firmly. His fingers were warm through the fabric of her blouse. "You should care, dear wife." He held her there for a tense moment. "Don't go just yet, honey. Let's talk about manners."

She craned her neck to look up at him, shading her eyes with her other hand from the bright sunlight.

He gripped her by the shoulders and pulled her close. "How much does it cost?" His mouth was drawn into a hard line, his jaw tense. She stared at the broad plane of his chest, her heart beating wildly in her chest. She didn't like being alone with him; she didn't like being this close to him. Her reaction puzzled her.

She hadn't felt anything strange when Romey had held her hands, instructing her in the dance, and he was pleasant looking. Then again, she wasn't afraid of Romey. That's all it was, fear. So she lied, a bad habit she was getting into around the man. "I don't understand what you are asking, Mr. Branton."

He cupped her chin and forced her to look at him. "I told you before, call me Nicholas. And I think you do. I just want to know, does a dance cost less than a tossing of your skirts in the gardens?"

Camille was so angry she could burst. The words were out of

her mouth before she could stop them. "You can't afford either."

21

His eyes grew darker. She noticed he hadn't shaved that morning; a graze of dark whiskers covered his jaw, making him more menacing. He wore a white shirt open at the neck, the sleeves rolled up, a pair of dark breeches, and suspenders.

He jerked her body closer and bent low to her ear. "Let me show you how the first is done."

"I don't want to dance with you."

"You should have thought of that before." He whisked her around forcefully, giving her no time to utter a reply, barely giving her time to keep up with him. He leaned low; he pulled her much too close; he brushed her nipple with his arm. He was in complete control. His touch was heated, his movements lithe and commanding. Her body had no choice but to follow his. Camille felt ragged and breathless, like a doll dragged around by a young child.

"Please," she whispered. "Please stop."

Nicholas stilled their movements but did not release her. She was trembling. He pulled her close, his arms slipping around her. He buried his face in her hair, then quickly brushed her lips with a kiss. She squirmed in his embrace, pushed at his chest.

"Don't struggle, love," he breathed. "I just want a small taste of what you give so freely to others."

He bent his head lower, angling her body against him. For one small moment, he forgot who she was. His mouth slanted firmly over hers, tasting her intimately.

Heat slid through Camille's body; her limbs trembled; her heart raced. She could feel the sculpted muscles of his thighs through the material of his breeches; the long, hard length of him pressed intimately against her. For one small moment, she forgot who he was and lent herself to the physical experience of the kiss. The roughness of his cheek brushing hers, the way his lips coaxed and commanded hers...it made her feel weak. The garden, the dance lesson, his hurtful words...it all slipped away as his tongue glided over her lips and into her mouth like water over a smooth rock.

His long fingers slipped over her breast and she gasped, trying to pull away from him and the foreign sensations he was creating in her body. But his lips were firm, persuasive. She didn't even know that she didn't want him to stop. But he chose that moment to do so.

He laughed, releasing her, and started to walk away. "That's how it's done, madame." Then he was gone.

Camille's lips were slightly swollen from the pressure of his kisses. Why had he done that? She felt shaky. Maybe he just wanted to teach her another lesson. He was toying with her again. Proving to her that he was in control, he was stronger and more experienced than she was. He was making the point that he would always win any little game she played with him.

He had walked away as if nothing had happened. Yet here she stood, utterly confused, her heart still beating uncontrollably in her chest. It made her even more determined not to show any emotion come the night of the party. She would graciously laugh, dance, and talk with other men, but she would not let Nicholas kiss her again. Nor would she be an adoring wife. What had Meagan called that rich woman who had come into the tavern in a snit, looking for her drunken, wenching husband? An *ice princess.* It was rumored the man came to the tavern seeking what his frigid wife would not give him. That's what she would be from now on. A frigid ice princess. She would remain limp and unmoved in his arms if he ever tried to kiss her again.

Camille gathered her courage and stomped off, choosing a separate path. The man himself could use a good dunking in the river. So could she, for that matter. She was warm all over. From the dancing, of course.

22

The ball had been an unimagined success for Camille but her nerves were taut and she was exhausted. It had all gone by so quickly. She was saying goodnight to a few guests when Camille saw Genevieve approaching and then the room started to sway. The next thing she remembered was coming to on the ballroom floor and hearing laughter. She stood up on shaky legs.

"Why are they laughing?" she asked, leaning on Genevieve and looking at the women who were laughing at her. "Fainting is usually a sign that you are carrying a child," she replied.

It took a moment for Genevieve's words to sink in. Then Camille felt a wine-colored flush sneak into her cheeks. "Oh," was all she could manage. She took a deep breath. "But it's not possible…."

"You're right, it's not. Not this soon anyway," Genevieve said. "It's my fault. I've pushed you into this too soon. Romey worked you hard and then tonight you've exerted yourself and you're tired. You did it all so well you exhausted yourself." *And if my brother didn't notice how you dazzled everyone, how beautiful and right you looked in his arms tonight, he's an absolute idiot,* she thought. "I keep forgetting this is all new for you." She winked, her dark eyes conspiratorial. "If it's any consolation, you were magnificent."

"I think I'd like to lie down. Is it proper etiquette to leave my guests now?"

"Forget about etiquette. You don't feel well. Besides, many of the guests will retire to their rooms after this dance. It's the last dance. You aren't expected to dance it with your husband."

Camille scanned the room, not seeing Nicholas. She frowned. If he was with *her*, that ostentatious, loud, gaudy, free-wheeling woman from the river boat, the one he'd danced three dances with, Camille would have words with him later. If she was going to play the part of adoring wife, he was going to act the part of adoring husband.

"You've fainted. No one would expect you to graciously say your goodnights…in your condition." Genevieve laughed softly. "It's the perfect excuse to slip quietly upstairs to your bedchamber. Let them think what they want. Go on…." Genevieve gave her a gentle push.

"Thank you," Camille said softly, making her way out of the ballroom and up the stairs. It had taken every ounce of courage and strength she had to pull off the charade. It was hard work being a lady. Truth be known, however, she had enjoyed every minute of it. Even the first cordial dance with Nicholas hadn't been too bad. He hadn't danced at all like he had when they'd been alone in the gardens. He had been proper, polite, aloof. Disinterested. Whereas, her very skin had felt like it was dancing, hot and alive, at his merest touch. The fear again. She thought she hid it well.

She had danced with several very attentive men; she had not danced with her hips or stepped on their feet or stained her gloves or uttered anything foolish. She had held her head high, lowered her lashes coyly, and laughed appropriately at their comments—amusing

or not. She'd learned a lot about the people attending the ball from

Romey beforehand. It was all she could do not to laugh when

Meredith Troutwine, a woman of formidable size trussed up in yards

of aquamarine taffeta, lifted her nose in the air and walked off as

Camille was introduced.

The woman tripped on the hem of her dress and fell over, rolling

to the ground like a stuffed sausage. Camille had graciously offered

her hand to help her up, despite the slight, and Meredith

begrudgingly accepted, looking quite mortified. Romey had told her

that one of Meredith's plump daughters had been quite taken with

Nicholas since she was thirteen, so perhaps that explained the

woman's animosity. The woman's daughter was still unmarried at

twenty and two, despite the family's considerable wealth, Camille

had been told. Genevieve had spent a good hour filling her in on all

the guests and their quirks before the ball had started.

Camille had not had time to worry much about Nicholas and

whether he had noticed—and approved—of her actions. She'd

noticed he danced with that woman three times, and rather closely at that. The woman was curvaceous, with glossy hair the color of midnight and gray eyes to match. Her dress was deep red and deeply cut, nearly exposing her ample bosom. Once, as Camille watched them dancing, she leaned very close to Nicholas and whispered in his ear. Nicholas had laughed at whatever she'd said. Camille had quickly turned her attention back to her dance partner.

As she tread softly up the elegant stairs, she wondered if he was with that woman now, enjoying the sorts of pleasures to which Camille was naïve. He had probably sauntered off to the city with her dances ago.

Absently, she trailed her hand along the banister as she wondered if he kissed that woman the way he had kissed *her* in the carriage. Did it always feel so…alarmingly warm?

As she expected, the door to Nicholas' bedchamber was open and the room was dark. She crossed through it to her room and softly shut the door, letting her eyes grow accustomed to the darkness. It was a beautiful warm night. She dug the pins out of her hair, letting it fall in waves past her shoulders, and opened the doors to the veranda. She stepped outside and inhaled the fresh air.

The moon hung in the blue-eyed night like shiny, wet silver. She could hear the soft rush of the river beyond. She felt irritated by the elegant gown she wore and carefully undressed, stepping inside to hang it in her wardrobe, removing her shoes and stockings, and then returned to the veranda in only her shift. No one was about; besides, her room was at the rear of the house.

It was very late. A welcome breeze ruffled her hair as she looked out over the gardens, trying to ignore the ache in her chest.

She found herself wondering about Nicholas, what he was like as a child, what he was like as a husband to his first wife. Had he played in these very gardens as a child? Had he known any moments of joy before he had become the hard, calloused man he was today?

She wondered about Meagan, about her uncle. She shivered as she thought of Meletios and wrapped her arms about herself. The thought of sinking into the soft covers on her bed and losing herself to sleep was very appealing. She stepped into the room and became still. The shadows were different. Or had they been that way when she'd come in?

Very slowly her eyes focused on long, lean legs crossed casually. Nicholas! He sat in the chair by the hearth, which was unlit at the moment. His voice slid out of the darkness, but she couldn't see his face.

"I only have one question, wife." He stood slowly and approached her, his eyes roving her small form and the thin fabric of her shift. He stood very close to her and lifted a thin strap from her shoulder, eyeing it with interest.

Camille trembled as his warm fingers found their way to her bare shoulder. "How long have you been in my room? I wasn't...." *Dear God, had he watched her undress?*

He laughed wickedly. Camille stepped back, trying to put some distance between them. "Did you purposely try to seduce our male guests tonight? You put on quite a performance."

"You were not pleased with my efforts? I was as gracious as I could be. I danced adequately." She looked at her hands. "I didn't stain my gloves and I wasn't rude to anyone, even when they were rude to me."

She walked away from him, cornering herself on the veranda. She presented her back to him, utterly hurt that he had not appreciated her efforts. "I tried to be what you wanted me to be, Nicholas. If it wasn't enough, I don't know what else you expect from me." Her shoulders sagged slightly.

He strode to the balcony, pinning her against the iron railing, one hand on each side of her. "Right now I don't care about gloves and decorum and dancing. I don't care how you learned it all so quickly, from whom, or why." He leaned close, his lips touching her earlobe. She trembled at the heated touch, which sent a dagger of warmth racing all throughout her body, stabbing her in parts she was unaccustomed to.

She prattled on, filling the tense silence with whatever came into her head. "I can't give you what you want. I'm not like that…woman you danced with three times, or the cultured young socialites who've attended these parties all of their lives."

"You're not listening, and I've tired of talk." His lips moved down her throat with practiced expertise, flooding Camille with new sensations. Why did his lips feel so good on her skin? Why was he kissing her tenderly?

The scent of sweet, aged brandy clung to him. He turned her in his arms, swept her up and carried her to the bed, laying her down gently.

He left her side for a brief moment and then stood at the side of the bed. He wore only his trousers, his magnificent bare chest corded with muscle. Camille clenched her hands at her sides. She felt such tension, such mixed emotions. Such...fright.

He leaned over her as if he would kiss her again then went still. In the wan light of the fire, he could see clearly the tears escaping from her big green eyes, fanning out over her golden lashes.

He turned from her and sat next to her on the edge of the bed. "Damn it, Camille. *Damn it.*"

She whispered so softly he almost didn't hear her. "You promised you wouldn't, Nicholas. You *promised.*"

He walked over to the hearth, keeping his back to her. He raised his arms and leaned against the thick marble, his head bent toward the flames.

Camille admired the broadness of his back, the strength of his arms, the leanness of his waist, the darkness of his hair that came just to the nape of his neck. Why did she itch to run her fingers through his hair, along his muscled flesh? It made no sense. She closed her eyes.

"You're right. I did promise. I don't know what came over me."

He kept his back to her. "Sleep well, madame. I will trouble you no more. Rest assured I will not be sleeping in the next room tonight. You've seen to that."

Then he was gone. She heard him angrily grab something from his wardrobe before the door slammed shut. She was alone, in a beautiful house with an army of servants. She had everything she could need, everything she had ever dreamed of—but it had come at a great price—the sacrificing of her dreams. She had an unlimited supply of clothes, an allowance; she didn't have to wonder where her next meal was going to come from. Yet she would trade it all for someone who loved her. And what had he meant, 'you've seen to that'? It was a long time before she drifted off to sleep.

23

Philip sprawled across the silk eiderdown, lazily smoking a cigar and watching Marlena, who stood half dressed at the window, her auburn hair unbound and wild about her shoulders, her bottom looking very spankable indeed. "Hoping for a glance of him, my dear?" he asked.

She turned to look at him, her small hand entwined in the long, silken draperies. The coldness in her eyes would've been a warning to any other man but not to Philip Branton.

It was humid, and the hair about her temples curled riotously. "Just enjoying the sights," she replied, turning back to the open window to watch the evening crowds below. "It's been so long, I'd almost forgotten what it was like here."

Philip laughed. "You're no good at lying, my dear. Never have been. You can't wait to see the look on his face. You're imagining how it will feel, aren't you? Admit it. You only need to be patient a little while longer."

He set the cigar aside and stretched, locking his hands behind his head. Lord but his brother's former wife was so transparent. Even now he knew she was impatient for tomorrow evening, when they would waltz back into his life. It was not because she had ever loved Nicholas, no. It was simply that she liked to shock people. There was nothing Lilliputian about her efforts. She hadn't ever cared a whit for Nicholas, or anyone else for that matter.

Philip and Marlena were very much alike. They knew what they wanted and they lived hard. He stared at the small rounded curve of her backside. Very spankable indeed. He grew hard at the thought. Still, when he finally did grow bored of her, he would simply walk away, as he had done so many years ago at Legacy Oaks.

His father grooming him all those years, building him up, expecting him to take over the family business. And now old Caindale was dead and had given everything to Nicholas, the son he had never cared for. Philip seethed.

It was laughable, really. Philip was not a man to settle down in one place. He preferred places like the French Quarter, unpolished places with shambling hordes of others just like himself, marauding through the narrow thoroughfares like they were playgrounds for the demented. The French Quarter was like a woman, a sultry, inviting, seductive, young woman with all the prerequisites of an alluring mistress when you first meet her.

It was late in the evening; the melancholy sound of jazz mingled with the sweet scent of ladies' perfume. Philip generally found most women foolish, imbecilic, their round bottoms in need of good spankings. Marlena had just happened to be married to his brother when they'd met and made love over and over in his room, her husband unaware and just doors away. She'd managed to last longer than any of the others. But the game was beginning to grow old. He hungered lately for a virgin, someone he could seduce and ride and toss away.

He'd thought about taking the pretty little maid servant who kept their rooms while Marlena ran her errands but decided against it for the time being. Still, keeping one woman too long was complicated, and Philip didn't like complications.

It had been easy to glean information about Caindale's death and his will; he and Marlena were staying in an out-of-the-way, elegantly furnished Creole townhouse just off the corner of Royal and St. Louis streets. It was owned by his old friend Madame Tussaud—an ancient, greedy hag who didn't care that he was back and who knew little of the Branton family dynamics.

Really, it was quite opulent with its great cupola, columns, and graceful archways, and Philip wouldn't have it any other way. He would have only the best.

They had the house all to themselves until the big evening approached, and indeed they'd made good use of the high-ceilinged, shuttered rooms, the crushed velvet blankets, Egyptian cotton linens, bathrobes to pad about in, and especially the four-poster beds draped in raw silk. He was still living off money he'd taken from old Caindale, though most of it had slid through his fingers by now. He enjoyed living lavishly, but the fact that his reserves were getting low was a bit troubling. He knew there was a way to get back what was rightfully his. Philip had never had any desire to *work* for a living, and didn't believe he should have to, whereas Nicholas had worked hard all his life, had had to manage wisely the stingy allowance Caindale provided him until now.

"We only have a few hours to plan our grand entrance," Philip said, more to himself than to Marlena as he watched a curl of silky white cigar smoke float toward the medallioned ceiling.

She flounced over to him and sat on the edge of the massive bed. "I know what to do," she said. He laughed at her calculated nature.

"What, my love, a tearful reunion? A duel?"

She purred, running a tanned, slender finger over the muscles in his chest. "Something better. Something that involves his prize horseflesh." Philip sat up. "Do tell me more."

"It's simple, really. As much as it kills me, I'll remain hidden for a while longer and you'll crash one of the Brantons' grand balls. You'll demand your rightful inheritance—the estates, the business, everything—in front of all the guests." She frowned, her eyes the color of smoked ash, her lush lips enticing. "Though his marriage to the chit does complicate things. But Nick is a proud man. Of course he'll tell you to bugger off."

Philip arched a golden brow, imagining the whole scene.

"Nick never could refuse a good race, now could he? And you're an excellent horseman, the best, in fact. You'll challenge him to a race, the prize being of course the estates. You'll let him choose the horse you'll ride, any one in his stables. He won't be able to refuse such a challenge in front of his guests."

"Your confidence in my skills is quite charming, my dear, but what if he does refuse? What if I don't win?"

Marlena bent down and licked his nipple, making it hard as her nails dug into the flesh of his golden-haired chest. She smiled wickedly. "He won't refuse and he *won't* finish the race, my dear."

"Whatever do you mean, my scandalous imp?"

"I've already arranged to have someone hiding in the bushes. When you round the last bend, hang back a little bit, but not enough to look like you're throwing the race. A shot will ring out. One that will end Nicholas' life and free you to step onto the scene and take everything, everything that was yours to begin with. The man is a very good mark. We won't be caught. It's foolproof."

"He damn well better be."

He picked her up and threw her down on the bed beneath him, driving his hard, hot shaft into her, not caring whether she was ready. She moaned with pleasure and spread her legs wide. When he was done thrusting into her and had come, she wrapped her slim thighs around his back and told him the rest of the plan.

After a respectable amount of time, she would reappear— claiming she'd been kidnapped and held against her will all this time, and of course, the two of them would fall magically in love. They could be married if it would make things look better, not that she cared for marriage or whether Philip took other lovers. All that mattered is that they would be back where they belonged—the rightful owners of Legacy Oaks—and Nicholas would be dead.

24

Nicholas had been away for two days and Camille found herself

bored. Lonely. Not having a clue as to what she should be doing

with her time. The gardens had quickly become a favorite escape of

hers, and as she walked in them, she was grateful for the haze of

sunshine after the recent rains. Everything glistened with a gold-

silver twinge of water drying in the heat.

Taking a seat on a marble bench she enjoyed a moment of quiet,

though of late, she did not like to be alone with her thoughts. She

hadn't seen Nicholas since the ball, since he almost....she didn't like

the train of her thoughts so she tried to think of something else.

But he was always there. Why couldn't she stop thinking about him? About the way his lips and hands had felt on her body? It wasn't fair, wasn't fair at all that *he* should evoke these feelings in her. The man who was her husband, the man who had promised he would never truly want her as his wife.

"Thinking about your new husband?"

Camille looked up in surprise to see Damaris standing by a boxwood hedge, her dark eyes sparkling, a malicious smile on her lips. There was knowledge in her eyes beyond her years, and Camille shivered, rubbing her arms.

"Would you care to join me?" Camille asked. She saw hesitation in the girl's eyes, but Damaris flounced over and sat down beside her.

"You know, Papa is often gone for long periods of time. I don't really miss him anymore." Though she had tried to disguise it, Camille had heard the catch in the child's voice.

"Never tell me you miss him," Damaris continued. "You're not even in love. Why did you marry him? You're just a tavern chit."

Camille sighed. "You're right, Damaris, and very astute. We did not marry for love. I think that's why people *should* marry, but often times they marry for convenience instead, and love never plays into it."

Damaris looked surprised. Camille knew the girl was still hurting over the loss of her mother, and now knew how she suffered from Nicholas' neglect. Camille focused on the fact that she was still a child, and that Camille wasn't, nor would ever be, a replacement for her mother—no matter how scandalous and uncaring Marlena may have been.

"Is that the best you can do, Damaris? Tavern chit? I mean really. I've been insulted by the best, and yours doesn't even come close."

"You're not…mad at me?"

"Heavens, no. It takes a lot more than that to make me mad."

Damaris thoughtfully chewed her lip. "You haven't answered my question."

"You're right. I'll be honest. I was forced to marry your father. It was arranged by my uncle. But I'll tell you something, Damaris. I didn't want to get married and I'm not trying to take anyone's place. I'm not your mother, nor will I ever be. And I won't pretend to understand your anger. But no matter how difficult you make things, I'm going to make the best of the situation. And I'd like to be friends."

"Friends? Ha! We don't have anything in common!"

Camille rose from the bench. "Don't we? I was even younger than you when I lost *my* mother." With that, Camille rose to go. She was not going to pressure the girl or tell her how to feel. She'd hated it when her uncle had done that to her. "It's up to you," she said over her shoulder.

25

"Oh stuff and bother!" Josephine exclaimed as the carriage bounced and rocked over yet another rut in the ragged road they were taking into town. She was attempting to pen a letter to her younger sister Caroline, who lived in London. What had possessed her to try to write in a carriage for God's sake?

Carrie, steadfastly opposed to the convention of marriage, and to the mere mention of the word itself, had reacted in quite a different manner to their father's dictatorial ruling of the household as they were growing up. She'd rebelled. Skipped across a continent, refused to bind herself to a man for support, took up educating herself, lived, God forbid, *alone* in a flat, and taught history and mathematics. Carrie had quite a brilliant mind. It wasn't that she didn't like men; she just didn't want to depend on one for any measure of happiness. Josephine smiled as she thought of Carrie smoking her cigarettes and beating most men at a gaming table.

In her latest letter to Josephine, Carrie had asked quite an intriguing question. Why, in God's good name, had Josephine endured twenty years of marriage to such a miserable cuss as Orvin Huxley?

Quite an intriguing question indeed. Orvin was a miser, surly from the day she'd met him, and, in the last two years of his life, had suffered a form of dementia that often led to embarrassing predicaments that Josephine handled with as much grace as she could. Pity was a horrible emotion to experience. Maybe even more horrible than loneliness.

She stopped trying to furiously stroke words onto the delicate egg-white paper set before her on the leather writing pad she'd had installed in the coach years ago. The strap to which the quill was attached was dangerously frayed. In fact, she wrote letters like a lunatic. It was a form of therapy for her. She didn't always send them; often, she simply stuffed them in the most convenient crevice; the décolletage of her gown, the pockets of her skirts, a desk drawer, the corners of the carriage, even the icebox, for God's sake. She was continually forgetting about them, finding them at some later date, and tossing them in the furnace like old newsprint.

Then she'd start another. Once she'd inadvertently shown up to a gilded affair with several scraps of paper sticking out from the bodice of her lavender, pearl-encrusted gown.

If the ride wasn't so bumpy she'd be writing about how you haven't lived until you've come upon your husband, clad only in his unmentionables, looking like an apple knocker, sitting on some poor unsuspecting family's front stoop quite out of his head. You haven't lived until you've wiped shit off of a 160-pound man who can't remember what purpose a chamber pot serves, or your name. Why indeed, she thought.

She'd visited him every day for an entire year right up to the day he died. Sat by his bedside in that God-awful institution, reading to him, adjusting his pillows or coverlet, bringing a glass of water to his lips. And every day, he either thanked her as if she were a stranger and not his wife of twenty years or cursed at her so vilely that she had to leave the room. Why indeed. She didn't know the answer. How unspeakably odious.

And yet she felt some sort of affection for him, she thought. But she suspected it had something to do with duty. He seemed to need her in an odd sort of way. As the elder daughter, Father instilled in her quite a fear of personal expression. She did her duty. Didn't question it. And now, looking back, she wished she hadn't lived the way she did. She wished she'd known she had choices.

She stared out the carriage window and wished she'd looked into her heart instead of locking it up. Her husband had hated everybody and everything. He rarely laughed. He spent most of the time in his apartments, surrounded by his precious shelves of snuff, beautiful jars with their gilt letters, and all the necessary apparatus for moistening and mixing; the snuff boxes he'd collected over the years. The only thing for which he ever felt any affection during the droll course of his life was his light-blue Sevres box.

And the way he talked…coxcombical…he screwed his mouth up and drawled forth his words and walked as if he had swallowed the kitchen poker. Oh, stuff and bother. It didn't matter now.

Josephine wouldn't waste any more time bellyaching. She had news

of such a nature she felt she would burst with joy. She was very

close to finding the granddaughter she hadn't known she'd had until

recently.

It brought tears to her eyes to know that a part of her dear

daughter had survived. "I am going to find her and when I do, I'm

going to make up for the all the terrible mistakes I made with her

mother," she said out loud. *I am going to make sure she knows that*

she has choices.

Josephine's heart ached with another kind of self-acquired but

much ignored knowledge she could only write in a letter to Caroline.

She wished she'd spent her life with a man who was affectionate,

a man who loved her down to the silly shape of her toes. A man

whose eyes would reflect love and admiration when he looked at her

and whose touch would be gentle and reverent and frequent, even as

she aged. Perhaps a silly wish for a woman of her age, she thought.

The carriage came to an abrupt stop in front of the offices of

Smith, Thiesen & Warner. The trio of detectives was among the best the city had to offer, and money was no object when Josephine had made up her mind about something. For the first time in her life, she was *glad* Orvin had been a miserable miser. Perhaps now she could finally put his money to good use.

She adjusted her elegant *capotte*, made of white crepe and satin and trimmed with fetching artificial flowers, and started on the first truly exciting adventure of her life in a very long time. She walked through the front door of the offices and felt a small thrill of hope.

26

The glass of wine Josephine had had after dinner went down so smoothly that she'd had another. And another. Feeling quite relaxed now, and slightly not herself, she decided she must speak with Henree. Surely she had something important to speak to him about. She couldn't quite remember what it was at the moment, but that didn't matter.

She trudged off to his apartments, which had always been separate from those of the other servants due to his elevated stature in the household, and felt the cool sting of wind against her cheeks. It felt good, as for some reason, she was overly warm.

She teetered down the path laced by the lavish gardens she'd recently had redone at great expense, and giggled. The moon was a slice of naked silver dangling in the sky like a jeweled bob in someone's ear. She was feeling quite the loon and didn't care.

She knocked on Henree's door and waited. No answer. Impatiently tapping her foot, which she was shocked to realize was bare, she raised her hand to knock again. The door swung open at precisely that moment and she fell inside, into a pair of strong arms, and for that matter, the bare, solid chest of the man. Giggling nervously, she righted herself and smoothed her hair behind her ears, which, Dear God, was also unbound.

Josephine couldn't seem to stare at anything but that broad muscular expanse of chest before her as Henree removed a pair of strange gloves from his hands. Boxing gloves. Slowly, she comprehended that the man had been boxing. His taut chest, sprinkled with a coarse, springy mat of dark and silver hair, glistened with sweat.

Well, the boxing explained why he was in such impressive physical shape. Josephine felt her cheeks flame and giggled again.

"Why Henree," she said, hiccupping, "I never knew you were a boxer."

She thought she saw a corner of his mouth lift slightly in amusement. He retrieved a shirt hanging from a peg on the wall and slipped it on, buttoning it. "My father was a pugilist," he said. "A very good one, in fact. Those are his gloves, actually. He had quite a bit of bottom."

Josephine crinkled her fine features in confusion. Henree was swaying just the tiniest bit. "He had a big bottom?" she asked. "And I say, do you have to move about so much? You're making me dizzy."

Henree laughed, a rich, delicious sound to Josephine's ears.

"Bottom means 'courage,' my dear. And I don't think it's me that's swaying. Are you...*flummoxed*?"

"I had a bit of wine after dinner, quite fine wine really, but I'm certainly not...I say, can I try that?"

"What, *boxing*?" Henree asked.

"Why not? It looks like it would be good for the...aggressions."

Silently, he handed her the gloves and helped her slip them on. They were outrageously big on her fists, of course.

"Now, place your feet apart, a little bit." He placed his hands on her shoulders and Josephine felt a delightful shiver of warmth. He stepped back. "Now hit me."

"Hit…you? Couldn't I just swing at the air or something?"

"Well, there's a lot of that in *unskilled* prize fights but that really isn't the point, my dear."

Josephine hiccupped again. "That's the second time you called me 'my dear.'"

Henree's cheeks colored slightly. "I'm sorry. It was inappropriate."

"Oh stuff and bother. I rather liked it."

"I…." At a loss for words, he said quickly, "You'd better hit me. Let's see if *you* have any bottom, my dear."

Wobbling, she took a step forward and swung. Completely missing him, of course, and toppling into his arms. Eyes locked. Breathing slowed. Pulses raced. Very, very gently, he placed a finger beneath her chin, caressing her cheek. They both tried to speak at the same time and laughed.

"Do you know what it's like to live with a man who doesn't desire you in the least, for twenty years?" she whispered. "To long for some small measure of affection before your heart truly dies from disillusion and loneliness and all your dreams die away too?"

She was studying the man's lips now and couldn't seem to take her eyes from them. They were so close to hers.

"Do you know what it's like to love someone from afar, for twenty years, knowing you can never have her for yourself?" he replied.

Abruptly, she stepped back from him as if she'd been sloshed with cold water. "I've been such a fool. I'm so sorry...."

"What are you talking about?" he asked, raking a hand through his dark hair, which was sprinkled, in the most masculine of ways, with silver along his temples.

"I shouldn't have come. I shouldn't have been so selfish. I've kept you in my employ, when quite clearly you've been in love with someone far away....

"Perhaps if I'd seen past my own unhappiness, considered someone else once in a while, I could've freed you from my employ, from the drudgery of serving me, so you could…so you could have gone to her and married her, and had a family of your own, and…."

"Madame, you don't understand…."

"Oh no, I see it all clearly now Henree. I am the veriest of fools. I must go now. Please, if you don't want to…stay on, I will understand. You must hate me for being so selfish, for making you cater to my needs all these years when I never, even once, considered yours."

She was crying now.

"But that's not it at all!"

"You don't need to be polite, Henree. If you decide…to leave in the morning, I'll understand. I'll pay you handsomely for all your years of service and then some. Oh dear," she muttered, flying out of his apartments in a whirlwind of white silk pajamas.

Henree rubbed his neck with his hand. The woman was blind. Incredibly, stupidly blind as to what he'd just confessed to her. Perhaps in the morning, after her head cleared, she'd dismiss him.

He opened the door and watched discreetly as she wobbled down the path in her bare feet until she disappeared into the house. She had very cute toes. Then he strapped on the gloves again. He felt dangerously close to crawling into some tavern and instigating a brawl. Dangerously, deliciously close.

27

It had been another wasted day. After walking in the gardens,

again, she made her way to her bedchamber. It was growing toward

dusk and Camille really wanted to talk with Nicholas. She was

growing impatient for his return.

He'd been away now for nearly a week. She needed something

to do, needed to find some way to be useful in his home. She

couldn't go on sleeping late every morning, wandering round the

gardens, doing nothing. It wasn't in her nature to be so idle. The

truth was she was used to serving people, used to tasks.

As she wearily climbed the steps, she thought of how to

approach him. She hated to ask him for anything, but she just couldn't go on like this. She would change for dinner and hope that he would arrive home. Afterward, she would talk with him. If he wasn't home for dinner, she would wait up for him again. It was that simple.

There was no need to fear him. Why was she so distraught about facing him, about asking him for something to keep her busy during the long, hot days?

She hesitated a moment before his bedroom door. It was closed. She could have sworn she had left it open this morning. Was he home? Should she knock? No, this was the only way to her bedroom and he had made it so. Without knocking, she pushed it open and was stunned by the sight that greeted her.

"Oh my dear, you must be lost. This is Nicholas' room, you know, the master of the house, the master of the boudoire, if you know what I mean?"

The woman lying in his bed in a filmy lavender night gown that left nothing to the imagination was beautiful. *The woman he'd danced with three times at the ball.* Her glossy black hair was unbound and fell wildly about her shoulders; her skin was near porcelain, her eyes the perfect mixture of blue and green and thickly lashed.

She pouted. "I am disappointed. I was hoping it would be Nicholas coming through that door." She ran a finger over the wine-colored silk eiderdown, her full lips in a pout.

Camille quickly composed herself. She felt drab next to the woman. She'd chosen to wear her own skirt and blouse and due to the humidity, a few riotous curls had escaped the braid hanging down the middle of her back.

Camille knew this woman was Nicholas' mistress—with her full, lush body and lack of shame she was the complete opposite of Camille. The anger and humiliation she felt was a shock; but years of working in a tavern with all kinds of inebriated and lecherous people had made her adept at controlling her emotions.

Quietly, she shut the door behind her so the servants would not hear the exchange that was about to take place.

"I demand that you leave his bedchamber at once." She crossed her arms over her chest and waited, tapping her foot.

What little color there was in the woman's pale skin drained away. She sat up but made no effort to cover herself. "This is rich. A tavern wench telling me to leave her new husband's bed. And what if I don't?"

Camille took a few steps toward her and the woman shrunk back into the covers. "You won't like the consequences."

The woman slithered out of the bed.

"Let's get something straight," Camille said. "I don't care if you're my husband's mistress. In fact, I don't care who you are or what you do when you're together." Neither woman heard the door open; they were so focused on each other. "I don't care if you continue to meet with him in private. It doesn't matter to me. But you will not do it *here*."

"I see you've met Lavinia." Both women turned at the sound of the male voice.

Camille raised her eyes to Nicholas'. She couldn't read what was in them. Displeasure? Doubt? Here she was, the unwanted wife tossing his mistress out on her ass.

"Oh Nicholas, it's so good to see you," Lavinia purred. "This insolent woman, your wife, was just telling me to get out. I can't believe it…a man like you with *her*…." She pouted. "Wasn't I good enough in bed?"

He put his hand up, not bothering to look at her. "Lavinia, get dressed and go downstairs. I'll be down shortly."

"But Nicholas…." He spared her a glance but said nothing more. She threw a robe on, gathered her things and strode angrily from the room, not caring who saw her in such a state of dress.

Nicholas was wearing a white lawn shirt, riding breeches, and boots. His boots and breeches were spattered with mud.

Camille turned to go but he reached out and grabbed her arm. "Not so fast, my dear. I'd like an explanation."

"*You* want an explanation? *I'm* the one who stumbled on your mistress, in our…your bed. I may be undesirable to you, Mr. Branton, but I am legally your wife and I won't be humiliated this way. We had an agreement."

His lips curled slightly at the edges, as if he found the whole situation amusing.

"You think this is funny? You forbid me to work in a tavern, yet you would break *your* word and flaunt your mistress beneath my nose? Everybody knows she's here. That helps create the image of the happily married couple, now doesn't it?"

He walked over to the bed, sat down, and began to remove his boots.

"What are you doing?"

"Getting changed for dinner, Mrs. Branton." His eyes—a heated gold—traveled over her attire very slowly, from head to toe. He had called her 'Mrs. Branton' with sarcasm dripping from his tongue. Her skin felt heated and warm where his eyes had touched her. "I hope you will do the same. I don't like you in that."

He began removing his shirt. Her lower lip trembled. Why should she care if he disapproved of her attire...or her looks? Just because he was incredibly handsome, impossibly so in the waning light of the afternoon shadows seeping through the shuttered windows....

"If that rude, irascible, bristly, cantankerous woman is staying for dinner, than no. I won't be joining you."

He laughed, his eyes a tawny glow. "You have quite a vocabulary for a…." He stopped mid-sentence.

"I know," she said sadly, not averting her eyes from his. "For a tavern maid. A thief. A whore. Isn't that what you were going to say?" She turned on her heel and quietly closed the door between their rooms, not wishing another word with him.

He was a neglectful father. A cold-hearted womanizer. A dreadfully handsome man who had stopped feeling things long ago.

As she flopped down on the bed and stared at the gold-flocked ceiling, she realized she didn't know who she was anymore. She didn't know how to be Camille Branton.

28

Genevieve was fond of parties. Camille barely had time to catch
her breath from the last party when she found herself elegantly
attired in a taffeta gown the color of ice and fanning herself from the
exertion of dancing.

Nicholas had danced the first dance with her, as was required,
but had not sought her company afterward. At dinner, Camille had
been seated between Martha and a handsome young man named
Billy Stone with blonde hair and friendly grey eyes. Across from her
was an engaging woman named Ruth Carver, a short, sturdy figure
in a black serge skirt and stiff white waist.

Her thick white hair was rebellious, her wit sharp. Dinner had been entertaining; Martha, Billy, and Ruth knew how to have fun, and Camille was sure she'd seen Billy's gaze directed longingly at Genevieve a few times during the course of the meal.

Now Camille was probably standing too close to the potted palms—she was practically standing *in* them, hoping to disappear—because she just wanted a moment to herself.

"Be my partner for the quadrille? That's next on the dance ticket." Apparently she hadn't hid herself well enough.

Camille turned to the gentleman who had approached her. She didn't recognize him. He seemed to have materialized from the shadows. She inclined her head and offered him her white-gloved hand. "We haven't been properly introduced, Mr....?"

"You'll find out soon enough who I am, Mrs. Branton." He didn't wait for the current dance to end but whisked her onto the floor. Taking her hand, they walked down the center of the floor as one of the pairs for the quadrille. The man who firmly held her arm had rakish blue eyes and chestnut brown hair with threads of gold, and he was tall—almost as tall as Nicholas.

"What do you think of your newly acquired husband, Mrs. Branton?" As they danced and turned around the large room decorated with mirrored walls, garlands of evergreens, and fresh flowers, Camille caught sight of herself in one of the mirrors and gasped. She almost didn't recognize the woman staring back at her, the woman dancing in the midst of such lavish decorations and handsomely attired gentlemen. There were whispers and murmurs all around them. A few women stared at them and covered their mouths with their gloved hands.

Flowering shrubs concealed the fireplaces and the musicians played from a balcony; a buffet of nectar jelly, Russian cheese, French bonbons, nougats, and cakes baked in fancy shapes now adorned the white cloth-covered tables. Truly, Nicholas had spared no expense.

"That's a rather personal question, isn't it Mr....you haven't properly introduced yourself." She'd noticed his easy British accent.

He laughed, leading the dance, commanding her steps easily. Camille noticed that a few young women watched them with envy. "No, I haven't, have I? But I'm not a proper sort of man, Camille.

187

Much like your husband. Now, tell me about what you think of him."

Flustered, she concentrated on the music, on her steps. "I haven't given you permission to call me by my first name. My husband is....well....I'm sure there are more interesting subjects."

He laughed, flashing a dazzling smile. "Do you love him?"

"You are forward, aren't you?"

"You haven't answered my question."

"It would not be appropriate to discuss such matters with a total stranger."

"Good. I'll take that as a no. Because if he doesn't want you, I do."

Camille stopped in the middle of the dance, not caring that she'd disrupted the other pairs, and abruptly walked off. When she turned and caught her breath, she saw the man's tall form retreating no doubt to the parlor for a drink with the other men who had declined participating in the quadrille. Perhaps that was where Nicholas was ensconced, for she hadn't seen him since the first dance. The rogue she'd just danced with was handsome indeed, and he'd stated he'd wanted her. It was a new feeling for Camille—a gentleman wanting her.

He wasn't as darkly handsome as Nicholas, but....she shook herself free from her delirium. The man was probably just toying with her. The thought saddened and infuriated her. Would people never get past the fact that she had worked in a tavern? Would they always think the worst of her, that she was an easy tumble in the hay?

Then she noticed Genevieve watching him too—and the look in her eyes was puzzling. Was it desire? Perhaps Genevieve knew who the rakish gentleman was.

29

"She passed the test, old chap," Kipp said.

Nicholas regarded him darkly. "What test?" He stood up, a bit wobbly on his feet.

"Pissant! You're drunk!"

"No, my dear friend, I'm not drunk, just delightfully oblivious," Nicholas replied. "What test?"

"She rebuffed me like a seasoned aristocrat. But I meant what I said to her. If you don't want her, I do."

Nick grabbed Kipp by the shirt collar and threw him up against the wall.

"Easy, Nick. I was just joking around." Nick let go of Kipp and poured himself another brandy. "Sorry, I don't know what came over me."

"She's gotten to you, eh?" Kipp said, pouring himself a brandy.

A hard look sprung to Nick's eyes and Kipp took a sip of the peach moby. "Hit a nerve, did I? Don't tell me you haven't bedded her yet."

He and Kipp were alone in the drawing room.

"If you'll recall, our agreement was to keep the marriage in name only," Nick scowled.

"Oh, I do recall, old chap. Quite a *conundrum* you're in."

"This is not funny."

"Who said it was? I feel interminably sorry for you. Having her so near, yet not able to reach out and touch her. God, she's beautiful."

"I think you've made your point." Nick shook his head. "But you're forgetting she's a whore and practiced at seduction."

"God, if she were my wife, it wouldn't matter who or what she'd been before. It would be fun to take her in hand, to roam my hands over that lithe, ripe little body...."

Nick looked dangerously close to assaulting him, but Kipp continued, enjoying it.

"You know, she was very gracious. And she just couldn't hide the joy in her face when she was dancing. Like every dance was the first. She's a joy, Nicky old boy."

Nick put his head down on the desk and motioned with his hand. "Go away. Just go away."

30

Camille walked the darkened hallway to her bedchamber. Having to pass through Nicholas' room every time she sought her own was ridiculous. She would have to talk to him about that. They weren't going to consummate the marriage, so what was the point of sharing a suite? Why couldn't she sleep in a different room, in a different wing? She felt caged, imprisoned.

She gently nudged his door open. It was dark. She sighed with relief and walked through it to her own room. Many of the guests had retired to their rooms. Nick was probably still in the study. Maybe he would sleep there, for God's sake.

That was another thing she wanted to talk to him about. His daughters and how he treated them. No, it was more a question of how he *didn't* treat them. Arabelle was sunny by nature, but both girls needed their father. Damaris, especially. She was deeply concerned about the state of Damaris' emotions.

Right now, Camille couldn't imagine the rest of her life. It was a blank, empty space, devoid of love, affection, and passion. That wasn't how she wanted to live. She wanted to have choices. She

wanted to wake up in the arms of a man who loved her. A man who

could teach her things, accept her for who she was. Nicholas

couldn't see beyond his own erroneous assumptions about her and

perhaps he never would.

She watched the soft flames dance in the hearth. Then she sat

down and wrote a short letter to Christopher. She'd kept his address

in a small crimson, cloth-covered box, her one extravagance, and she

retrieved it now. She sealed the letter and put everything back in the

box. Tomorrow she would take it into the city and she would visit

Meagan.

A shaft of waxy gold moonlight poured through the open doors

of the balcony, bathing the standing mirror in shimmering,

opalescent light. Camille undressed and stood before it. Scandalous

behavior, but no one was about.

She thought of Lavinia, her lustrous black hair, her full curves,

as she traced her fingers over her own breasts, the curve of her waist.

Her breasts were small but firm; her hips slim. She wondered how she would compare to Lavinia, what Nicholas would think if he saw her this way.

You're nothing but a skinny, stupid wench. Her uncle's words echoed in her head; he'd told her often enough.

It was true she'd filled out in the past year and a half, but he wouldn't have noticed because she hid it well beneath her baggy clothes. Still, she felt less of a woman as she thought of the practiced curve of Lavinia's full lips, the way her full nipples had strained against the exotic lavender lingerie she'd worn, the way her ample hips seemed inviting. The thought that Nicholas may have purchased the beautiful lingerie for her caused an unexpected ache. Then there was the full tilt of Lavinia's lashes, the unbound glory of her long black hair.

Camille unbound her hair. It was the complete opposite of Lavinia's. Somewhere between the color of honey and the color of wheat, and it hung to her waist. Her eyes were blue-green, and always seemed to be changing. Sometimes they were the color of the sky and sometimes the color of the sea.

She was slimmer than Lavinia, her movements awkward and innocent as she touched herself. Her nipples were pink and hardened as she put her hand between her legs, wondering what it would feel like to have a man touch her, to have Nicholas touch her....

There was a strange ache in her lower body, a strange sense of unbearable heated need.

Startled by the turn of her thoughts, she quickly threw a chemise over her head and turned from the mirror.

We are completely unsuited, madame. Now it was Nicholas' words that rang in her head. She climbed into bed and pulled the covers up to her chin, wondering what had gotten into her. The man was a devil. A hard-hearted seducer and womanizer who didn't believe in any of the things she believed in. Love. Marriage. Standing against the world *together*. It was a long time before she closed her eyes.

31

Despite the large quantity of brandy he'd imbibed, Nick slugged

back another glass. It had been a mistake of utter proportions to

retire to his bedchamber. He'd thought for sure his wife would be

asleep. He slid the gold wedding band off his finger and laid it on the

desk, as if the act could somehow distance himself from the woman

he'd married, from what he'd seen in the dark, moonlit shadows of

her room.

He was swollen and painfully hard beneath his trousers; his

mind was befuddled. Seductive, erotic images that could only be a

trick of the mind danced in his head. Shadows weaved unsteadily in

his study and he sat down, the leather chair creaking loudly. Rain tapped on the roof. *Drummed* the roof. Damn lot of rain lately, he thought. The bottle of brandy was two thirds empty.

He thought again of how Camille's door had been slightly ajar; he'd watched as she'd plucked at her skirts, unbound her hair, then stood naked in front of the mirror. In the moonlight, he had no trouble seeing what she was seeing. Against his will, as he watched her touch herself, he imagined what it would be like to hold her through the night, to feel her sweet curves pressed against him, to wake her sleep-washed form and make love to her, over and over.

He barely breathed as she ran her fingers over her small firm breasts, tucked them between her legs, closed her eyes. Then she'd frowned and thrown the chemise over her supple, slim body. He'd held very still, uncertain of himself in a way he didn't like.

A sliver of guilt ran through him. He'd behaved like an ogre. The worst kind of rogue. An idiot. He didn't like knowing he was responsible for her unhappiness. Yet he couldn't deny what he was feeling. Raw, naked desire for a woman who wasn't what she seemed.

Still, he wouldn't force himself on any woman, even his *lawfully wedded wife*. He'd quietly retreated to his study and his brandy. He cradled his throbbing head in his hands. He wanted to kiss her again. No, he wanted far more than a kiss from her. The last few weeks had been hell knowing she slept in the room beside him. He'd tossed and turned long into the night, his body hard with need.

His dreams were erotic, a place where he knew her body as well as his own. He teased her breasts with his tongue; he buried his fingers and then his hard shaft in her silken core, which was damp and sweetly wet. And she moaned while she stroked the air with his name, over and over.

We are completely unsuited madame. His words came back to haunt him. Sometime later, he simply fell asleep in his messy thoughts.

32

Camille woke with a start. After trying to get back to sleep, she simply gave up and wandered downstairs, drawn to the wan light slipping beneath the door of Nicholas' study. The door was slightly ajar, but Camille knocked anyway. No response. She nudged it open and her eyes met Nicholas' eyes.

He looked dangerous—bleary-eyed and rumpled. He hadn't shaved so his jaw was darker than it normally was, giving him a strong, menacing appearance. In that moment, he looked like a man who deliberately punished himself by deliberately putting himself in harm's way every chance he got.

His mouth was drawn into a grim line. He rubbed his eyes, then blinked. "You're still here," he said. His words were slurred. "I can't be sure if I'm dreaming."

Camille's stomach was churning. She could only push this man so far, and perhaps now was not the best time to do so.

He straightened but did not stand up. "Please, have a seat."

He started to pour another drink then stopped, glass mid-air. "Who the devil are you? I can't seem to figure you out," he asked.

Camille was sitting with her hands folded in her lap. She didn't want to meet those tawny eyes again but couldn't help herself. She wished she hadn't. His shoulders were thrown back, rigid with tension.

"Who...am I?" She frowned in confusion. "I...perhaps I should come back later. You seem...to have had a lot to drink." She rose.

"Don't."

She froze then sat down again.

"What is it you want at this ungodly early hour, Camille?" He raked a hand through his disheveled black hair.

"I couldn't sleep. I wanted to talk to you about Arabelle and Damaris."

He raised a wicked dark brow. "Indeed?"

Camille curled and uncurled her fingers in her lap, dropping her gaze again. "Well, yes. You see...."

"No, I don't. Please, enlighten me."

She should probably just leave. The man was practically snarling at her. Was she out of her mind? This really wasn't a good time.

She stood, resolutely this time. "I'm afraid I've disturbed you at a bad time, Mr. Branton. I'll come back in the morning."

She had almost reached the door when he put his arm out to keep her from opening it. "No. I'd like to hear what you have to say. *Now.*"

She was in an even worse position. She leveled her gaze at his chest. Another mistake. His shirt was open, revealing his taut skin and corded muscles. She couldn't think. "I...think...perhaps you could spend more time with them. Especially Damaris. Her emotions...."

His arm snaked around her back. It was unyielding. He watched her lips, but he didn't seem to hear what she was saying.

"You aren't listening Mr. Branton. I…."

He couldn't fight it anymore. All his life he had tried to win his father's affections. All his life he had promised himself he wouldn't be like Caindale Branton. But somehow, somewhere, he'd started turning into the man. Hard, unyielding, taking what he wanted. And right now he wanted Camille. Situation be damned. He couldn't help who he was.

His arm tightened about her waist like a band of steel. That kiss they'd shared in the gardens had been so incredibly sweet and unguarded. He wasn't a man to desire a woman so…intensely. And why, for the love of God, did it have to be *her*?

He wanted to snatch her against him, feel the ripe litheness of her body pressing into his, and by God, he would.

His mouth descended with alarming quickness. Vaguely, in some far off region of his brain, he realized she was fighting him, trying to twist away from him. He ground his hips against hers. "Easy, love," he breathed. "Don't fight it."

He tasted her with his lips, his heat, his eagerness. She broke the kiss for a moment and he heard her sharp intake of breath. "Is this to be a punishment then, for speaking my mind?"

He laughed wickedly. "Punishment? No. Pleasure? Yes." His mouth descended again and Camille lost all train of thought. His mouth was moving over hers with such sweet tenderness that heat spiraled and throbbed between her legs. She was powerless to resist the warmth of his lips, the tantalizing teasing of his tongue.

Dear Sweet God, but she wanted desperately to feel the strength of his arms about her, the brand of his mouth on hers. He led her to a settee nestled in the crook of the window, awash in the translucent light of summer moon.

He stared at her as he slowly undid the buttons of her simple blouse. Then he pushed it off her shoulders slowly, very slowly, pressing his lips to her soft flesh. He bent his dark head to her breast. The shock of his warm mouth on her nipple made her feel like her soul was splintering.

The sight of him there, the rough, raw feel of his whiskers against tender skin, caused a delicious throbbing everywhere in her body. She put her hand on his chest. Warm skin. Thudding heart.

She didn't realize he'd rolled down a stocking until it was discarded at her feet and she felt his large hand resting intimately on the top of her thigh. So close to that part of her that no man had ever touched....

Never had she felt so warm and feverous. She tried to speak. She tried to sit up, but he was half lying atop her. "It's alright." His lips found their way to her mouth again. She tried to keep her legs together but he wouldn't have it.

"Open your legs for me," he said.

His voice in the dark was a raw scrape of whisper that stroked her to the core. Gently but firmly he pushed her legs far enough apart to stroke her with his finger. She gasped. "Nick...."

He plunged a finger inside and she arched her back in pleasure.

"That's the first time you've used my name. God, you're so wet, so tight."

He continued to move his finger, slowly, then with more urgency. "I…what's…."

"Just let it come, love," he said.

Soon she was writhing in ecstasy, a warm heat spiraling through her entire being, her soft flesh clutching and convulsing around his finger. And then there was nothing but fire, flashes, sweet, almost unbearable release.

He removed his shirt and Camille stared. His shoulders were wide and strong, the muscles of his arms smooth and tight. Vaguely, she was aware of her thoughts. Why this man? Why him? She looked into his eyes and was reminded of the gold light of the sun caressing desert sand. Her heart thundered in her chest; she couldn't slow her breathing. The ache started again as she watched him undo his breeches.

She stared at him in wonder. She'd never seen a man before. He was large, rigid, and…leaning against the base of her womanhood! Fear curled in the pit of her stomach. An irascible voice whispered inside her head, *what are you doing?*

"Don't! Please," she whispered. "Don't hurt me."

Nick felt like he'd had a bucket of cold water dumped on his head. Was he out of his mind? What the hell was he doing?

He stared at her lovely flesh, the silken golden-haired pink part of her that he wanted to sheath himself inside, watched as she bit her lower lip, then quickly stood and dressed. She pulled her dress down to cover herself.

She drew a deep breath. He looked so angry.

"Hurt you?" he snarled. "I lost my head. It was the drink. I forgot you've been ridden by more men than the racehorses in my stables."

His words stung and twisted themselves deep in her heart. She tried not to cry, but the tears spilled freely down her cheeks. Red-faced and thankful for the darkness, she adjusted her clothing.

She stood, seeking to step around him, only to find herself snared by the elbow and whirled around to face him. She flung up her hands between them. "Let go of me!"

His smile had vanished; in its place was a cruel frown. "And by the way, how I conduct myself with my daughters is no concern of yours."

"It surely is! I'm your wife. I will never take the place of their mother, but they *need* you. They're still hurting from losing Marlena. My God, can't you see it?"

He let her go and she practically tumbled away from him. She blinked furiously as more tears stung her eyes. Her shoulders slumped. "You are the most stubborn man I've met. I'm going home. I won't be treated like this."

"Where will you go? You have no home. This is your home now."

As soon as the words left his mouth, Nick knew it was the wrong thing to say. The sadness that leapt into her green eyes, the way she held herself, it was as if he'd physically struck her. He'd been prepared for her outrage, for fiery, scorching words. But not for this. Not for her sobbing, as if her very heart were broken.

"You're right, of course. I have no home now," she said quietly. "I have no one." Then she was gone.

33

Camille had successfully avoided Nicholas for a week now. She'd spent time with the girls, not as much with Damaris as with Arabelle, but she'd made progress. She truly cared about them and their well being, and she thought she was getting through, even if it was slow progress.

She'd made a habit of going to the stables and riding every day; the exercise was exhilarating. And she'd been to see Meagan twice. Meagan's bruises were healing nicely. She hadn't wanted to, but Meagan had finally accepted the money Camille had saved, all the money Nicholas had given her since she'd married him. Camille didn't need it; she didn't need things for herself. And now Meagan didn't have to work in the tavern. In fact, she had returned home and was trying to patch things up with her parents. Meagan would never have her little girl back, would never again hold her in her arms or kiss her little soft cheeks, but perhaps she could start healing, somehow.

Camille was working up the courage to ask Nicholas if she could invite Meagan for a visit. She felt like she shouldn't have to ask, she should just go ahead and invite her. But Meagan had been through so much, if Nicholas reacted negatively, she didn't want her friend to experience that.

She'd even managed to mail the letter to Christopher. She didn't know how long it would take to reach him; she only hoped he would come for her once he got it. The thought got her through the long days, the self doubt, the tangle of thoughts she'd been having about Nicholas. Each time she thought about that night in his study, imagined his dark head bent possessively over her breast, sucking and teasing it, she felt her cheeks flame at the intimate memories. She felt like she was moving in a dream. Unsure of herself, of her place.

She'd been walking in the gardens and was heading back to the house, near the stables, when she heard the thundering beat of a horse's hooves. Kipp Gresham came riding into the yard, dismounted, and handed the reins to a stable boy. She'd learned his name since the night of the ball. He was the one who'd danced with her and asked her such forward questions.

"Camille," he said. "What a pleasant surprise."

She was wearing her own skirt and blouse again, and getting tired of washing it out so often, but she couldn't yet bring herself to wear any of the fancy things Nicholas had had made for her. Kipp smiled rakishly.

"Mr. Gresham."

"Nicky and I were going to go hunting today, but he seems to have misplaced his shotgun."

Camille frowned.

"Oh, not a fan of hunting, are we?"

"To tell you the truth, I find it barbaric."

Kipp smiled. "Most women do. Must be something wrong with us men. And please, call me Kipp. Have you seen Nicky about?"

"I haven't seen him for…I don't know where he is right now, Kipp."

Kipp beamed at the use of his first name. Camille hoped he wouldn't read anything into it. She couldn't even bring herself to call her husband by his first name, for God's sake. It was too…intimate. It didn't feel right.

They continued to walk through the flower-ribboned paths to the house.

"Are you excited about the annual Branton summer soiree?" he asked.

Camille pretended to know about it. "The Brantons are very fond of parties, aren't they?"

"You haven't seen anything yet, Camille. Just wait. Four hundred guests, fireworks, horse racing, dancing, the most spectacular spread of foods you will ever see in your life. Not to mention the most handsome bachelors, like myself." He winked.

His charm was infectious. Camille caught herself wondering what Nicholas was like in his unguarded moments.

"Indeed, why hasn't a charming man like yourself found a bride-to-be yet?"

"Because he's a rogue of utter proportions." Both heads turned at the sound of the deep voice. Nicholas stood in the doorway, his arms crossed over his chest. "Trust me, he wouldn't make a good groom."

Camille was struck by his dark, good looks. He looked refreshed, his skin golden tan, his eyes dancing with mischief, his shoulders impossibly wide. As usual, she couldn't read his mood. And she knew it could change in a second.

"Speak for yourself, old chap."

"I still haven't found the shotgun," Nick said.

"No matter," Kipp replied. "I didn't come to see you."

Nick frowned, clearly puzzled. He looked from Kipp to Camille.

Genevieve pushed her brother gently from behind and stepped around him.

"Ready Kipp?"

Nicholas looked disturbed. "Oh no, now wait a minute. That's my little sister."

The carriage was brought out and Kipp helped Genevieve inside. "Don't worry old chap. She's in good hands."

"She better come back with every single hair in place."

"We'll see, old chap. We'll see."

Camille was smiling triumphantly. She'd guessed right. Kipp had a soft spot for Genevieve. Maybe she was the woman who would tame his rakish ways.

"What are you smiling about?" Nicholas said, clearly annoyed.

Camille ignored his remark. She crossed her arms over her chest and tapped her foot impatiently. "And just when were you going to tell me about the four hundred guests we'll be having?"

"Bloody hell. I was getting around to it."

She held her chin high as she walked around him into the house. But she couldn't hold back. "You know, Mr. Branton, you can't tell someone not to fall in love with your sister. It doesn't work like that."

"And you would know about love, wouldn't you, my dear?"

She stopped, turned and glared at him. "You uppity, arrogant, conceited, goat-headed, vainglorious cock!"

214

She felt her cheeks flame. He was at her side in two long strides.

He pulled her roughly against him. "Maybe you shouldn't give advice about things you don't understand."

Arabelle came dancing into the room and they quickly separated.

"Which dress should I wear for the party, the green one or the blue one?" she asked. She held them up and looked expectantly at Camille.

"You would look positively stunning in either," Camille said, "but I think I prefer the green. It brings out your beautiful dark eyes."

Nicholas chose that moment to escape.

34

At dinner that night, it was just the two of them. Quite uncomfortable. Genevieve was dining in the city with Kipp; the girls had eaten earlier.

"Where did you learn to ride?" Nicholas asked Camille.

"A kind old man who owned a stable taught me. He let me ride with his daughters sometimes."

"You ride passably well," he remarked, taking a hunk of bread and slathering butter on it.

Camille took a sip of wine to steady her nerves. Nicholas' dark hair fascinated her as well as the gold light in his eyes. His shoulders filled out his dark navy jacket and his rugged jaw looked like it could be hewn of stone. It was a strong chin; it could harden in an instant.

"I know a lot about horses," she said. "You'd be surprised."

"Ever race one?" he asked.

"Race one? Heaven's no. But I know it takes a special person to tame one. Horses aren't troubled by a whole lot. They don't care about how they fill their time. All they care about is their appetite and trust. They can smell fear."

Nicholas put down his fork and came to stand beside her. He placed his hand on hers.

"I've been thinking," he said. "That maybe we should start over. Start...again."

Camille tipped her head to look up at him. "What?"

His fingers were warm and pleasant.

"I mean, I haven't been...very pleasant to you. I'd like to get to know you a little better."

He reached out and brushed a tendril of smooth hair from her cheek.

Camille wasn't sure what to think. She blurted out the first thing that came to mind. "Why?"

He laughed and gestured for her to stand. She stood and he took her by the arm to the wide windows overlooking the gardens and several pastures. "I'd like to call a truce."

"Mr. Branton, this is unexpected. I...."

"You could start by calling me Nicholas. Actually, I prefer Nick."

Camille stared out the window, focusing on the beautiful green pastures viewed from this part of the mansion, the wide blue sky. "I guess that wouldn't be too hard, if we could talk about me getting my own room, so I don't have to go through your room every time.... I mean...."

He frowned. "That can be arranged. Though it will make the servants talk unless we convince them it is because you need a bigger room."

An older stable hand led a beautiful white horse into the pasture. In her excitement, Camille gripped Nicholas' arm. "Oh my God! What a beautiful horse! I didn't know you had an Arabian."

"I didn't. Until yesterday. She's a new addition to the stable."

The horse was so white she was almost silver under the smoky blue sky. "What's her name?"

Nicholas smiled. "I think you should name her."

"Me? But...."

"She's yours, after all. A gift. I've never given my wife a gift."

Camille swallowed, feeling the hot ache of joyful tears in her throat. "A gift? I can't possibly accept it."

"Well, I can't give her back. Someone has to ride her."

The horse was as pale as powder, her eyes dark as ash. "I'll call her 'Passion.'"

"I like it."

They returned to the table and Camille talked shyly for the rest of the meal. She didn't know the man sitting across from her, his many moods, his many faces. She drained a glass of wine and then summoned her courage.

"I know you hate me for ruining your life. I know you didn't want to marry. You wouldn't have had to if it wasn't for your father's will."

He put his glass of wine down and looked into her eyes. His eyes darkened. "My life was ruined a long time ago, and not by you."

"But now you're even more…miserable."

He laughed. "How do you know I wasn't *always* this miserable?"

She took a deep breath. "I don't think you're that kind of man." Inhale. Exhale. Again. "In the short time I've known you I think you are the type of man who wouldn't appreciate anything unless he had to fight for it."

He stared at her. His eyes were clear and direct. "I think you are far more miserable than I."

She fingered the edges of the lace napkin in her lap. "You must hate me."

"Truly, Camille, I do not hate you."

He looked at her face. Her skin was flushed; her eyes were a darker blue than he'd ever seen before. "We haven't tried to make this situation more…tolerable, have we?"

She shook her head.

"Perhaps we should," he said.

"But…I'm not any of the things you would ever find desirable in a…wife." She had trouble getting the word out and over her lips.

This was crazy, insane. She was no different than Marlena, his head admonished. *They did not suit.*

"I would be willing to try," she said softly. "If it would mean a more peaceful household," she added quickly, feeling happier than she had in a long time. "There are the girls to think of."

"OK then. Would you consider riding with me tomorrow? You could ride Passion."

Camille grinned. "I accept your invitation."

Nicholas would be racing in a few days, as part of the gala summer celebration. He had hoped that Camille would be there cheering him on. *The heart is a funny thing*, he thought. *Why should he care?*

35

The massive, rambling house was now full of handsomely dressed guests; there were heavily laden food boards, good talk, and laughter. Camille had a feeling that the Branton family would go on for a long time in this way.

As guests arrived in the great hall, they would pull off their hats and gloves. They seemed to be spilling out of every crevice of the house.

The hall was slashed deep into the big house and double doors opened off it at regular intervals along each side. It was high-ceilinged; the walls were of light-colored wood, beautifully grained and softly polished, and the floor was now covered with a rich, red carpet that shimmered like the folds of a gown.

The fireworks display would begin later, and the children were at peak excitement. Arabelle had told Camille all about it—there would be small Chinese crackers, cannon crackers, skyrockets, and Roman candles.

Camille felt radiant, maybe for the first time in her life. She felt light and joyful, and found herself looking for Nicholas in the throngs. Her hair was as polished as a piece of gold satin; it was carefully imprisoned with small jeweled pins that held it back from her face, but the rippling, waving mass escaped in a pile of curls at the back of her head. Her skin glowed, her cheeks were highly flushed. Her eyes were blue-green and heavily lashed, her lips full and sweet.

Her gown, of gleaming, rustling, very fine raspberry silk, was made for her white-skinned beauty, or so Genny had told her. She and Genevieve had become friends and Camille enjoyed using her nickname.

A black velvet ribbon ran through the lace edging about the low necklines of Camille's dress. Her small waist, above the flaring hoopskirts, was tightly laced and also encircled by a black ribbon. She wore small black satin slippers beneath the wide skirt.

She found herself wondering if she would meet with Nicholas' approval. She moved out into the crowds gathered on the vast, stretching green lawns, greeting guests and occasionally stopping to talk to someone. There was still no sign of Nicholas.

Camille moved off to the side, near the base of a wide old oak tree. She scanned the crowd and her eyes rested on Nicholas. For an instant their glances crossed and she lowered her lashes. He crossed the distance between them quickly, carrying two glasses of champagne in his hands.

He offered her one and she took it. "Thank you."

He stared at her. She was a completely different woman than the one who had stood in his study that first day, dirty and tattered. She was innocence and sensuality, and dangerously lovely.

"You are…captivating."

Camille blushed. "And you are…." She laughed. "I don't know who you are."

He smiled. Then he took both glasses and set them down. His eyes traveled leisurely down her form. "I'm looking forward to being the first to dance with you tonight."

Camille didn't know what to make of it. He stood close to her, so close she imagined she could feel his muscled chest.

They had attracted attention. "We're being watched," she said shyly. Her gaze caught his.

"Let's give them something to talk about then," he replied.

Music floated in the jasmine-scented air and he took her in his arms and began to dance.

Camille felt giddy. She laughed lightly.

This was dangerous. She should be careful. It wouldn't do to lose her heart to a man who had promised never to truly desire her.

"Were you always drawn to the sea?" she asked.

He leaned close, his breath a hot whisper against her ear. "There will always be men who follow the sea," he answered. "The best seamen love a fast ship. I've seen clippers take tea cargoes out of

Chinese ports for England because they're fast, while British ships wait at the docks for weeks on end. I've always loved the water, the open sea. I want to control the triangle trade—west to north to south, then south to north to England. But it's difficult to secure crews for coasting vessels."

"You plan to…sail again soon?"

"I need to take a short run to Charleston, yes."

His lips brushed her ear. "Will you miss me, my sweet?"

Liquid threads of heat spindled through her body.

Camille felt like she was dreaming. She didn't have time to answer him.

"My, you two are certainly cozy."

They brought their heads up at the same time, without separating.

"Lavinia," Camille said. "I trust you're enjoying the party?"

Lavinia was dressed in a drop-dead gorgeous rustle of crimson silk, her black hair a marked contrast to her white skin. Her eyes were grey and heavily lashed; her lips red and full and perfectly molded into a seductive smile.

"Not as much as you, my dear." Her eyes boldly assessed Nicholas' tall form.

Camille felt the flush rise to her cheeks.

"It's no wonder he's being so nice to you now, dear. I'd be happy too if I'd married for that kind of money. Imagine."

Lavinia turned, her silk skirts rustling, and Nicholas swore beneath his breath. The newspaper gossip column. He'd forgotten about it. Another article had appeared and he'd meant to show it to Camille, to ask her about it.

Camille withdrew quietly from his embrace. "What is she talking about?"

He gripped her arm firmly. "I think we should discuss this in *private*," he said, raking the other hand through the midnight terrain of his hair.

She nodded and he led her through the crowds to his study. While she seated herself, he poured two more glasses of champagne. Silence mounted. He handed her a newspaper that was lying on his desk and sat down.

Her heart lurched; he was staring at her oddly. "I don't put much stock in rumors, Camille. You shouldn't either."

Her eyes scanned the article and her heart beat a little faster. For a moment, everything was forgotten except the words on the page:

Josephine Huxley, a wealthy widow, is asking for the public's help in finding the girl in this photo. She would be 18 now. It turns out that the girl is her granddaughter and heir to the Huxley fortunes....

The newspaper was three days old. That would mean....

"What is this?"

"I don't know," Nicholas said. "I thought maybe you could tell me."

"When were you going to tell me about this?"

"It's just gossip, Camille." The glacial coolness had returned. "I'd forgotten about it."

"The girl in that photo *is* me. It…the photo, it was taken shortly before my parents died. I remember because it was the photo they ran in the newspaper after the accident…."

She took a sip of champagne. Then another. "But…I don't have a living grandmother that I know of…."

"Is it possible you were adopted?"

Camille wasn't listening. *Three days ago*, she thought. That's when he'd made a peace offering, given her the horse. Was it because he thought there might be some truth to the rumor? That she was worth…what had the paper reported…*hundreds of thousands of dollars?*

What a fool she'd been. Was Nicholas in financial straits? It didn't seem so, with all the lavish parties. But still….

Too hurt to speak, she looked at her lap. There was an air of danger about her husband that alarmed her. "If it should turn out to be true," she breathed, "would it change your opinion of me?"

"No," he said bluntly.

"Have you…been with Lavinia since…since we called a truce?"

His fingers tensed around the crystal glass. "What does it matter?"

That was all the answer Camille needed. Oddly, to hear no denial that Lavinia had been in his bed burned her insides, made her ache in a strange, foreign way.

"It doesn't matter," she said quietly. "I understand the ways of men and their promises, Mr. Branton. Their smooth tongues, their golden words, their lies." She struggled to hold back the tears in her eyes. "If that is to be the way of our marriage, then I assume you shan't object if I should decide to have a gentleman caller," she said, thinking of Christopher.

He came around the desk so fast she thought he would knock his champagne glass over.

He hauled her out of the chair, his arms grasping her firmly. "We *are* wed," he seethed.

"Yes, I know, I am the wife you didn't want, the wife you had to take to honor your father's wishes.

"But I need to remind you that we are *both* wed, Mr. Branton, and I will not be held to a different standard merely because I am a woman. Therefore, you will mind your manners and your tongue!"

"I'll not have you making á spectacle of yourself, running wildly about town with any man you choose."

"If it were up to you, you'd keep me locked up in this house!"

Camille stared into his eyes. "Are you *jealous*?"

He smiled wickedly, coldly. "No, my lady. But if I decide to have you, I'll be the only man for you."

"I will remind you of our bargain."

"I need no reminding," he said, his voice raspy.

Camille had mocked him and she was appalled at her boldness. Why had she taunted him so? She wanted to be rid of him—and he of her. Yet, Sweet God, she wanted to feel his strong arms around her, wanted him to kiss her again, wanted him to touch her...."

She fought to clear her head, to think rationally, not to think of the searing brand of his lips on hers.

"If you won't banish Lavinia from this house, from your *bed*," she breathed, "if you continue to humiliate me, I shall do as I please.

231

I shall stay out until all hours of the night; I shall visit the tavern; I shall have gentlemen callers."

His eyes narrowed dangerously.

"I won't allow it."

"You shall forbid me?"

"You will not stay out until dawn, nor will you visit the tavern, or any tavern, or have any gentlemen callers in *this* house."

"You can't stop me."

"Oh, madame, I can and I will."

"What will you do, lock me in my room?"

"If that's what it takes."

"Oh, just let me go!" She jerked from his embrace and he stepped back, his face expressionless.

He turned his back to her to retrieve the entire bottle of champagne. "Trust me, dear wife, you don't want to do battle with me."

When he turned to face her, his chin had hardened. His eyes were narrow gold slits.

"Tell me Mr. Branton," Camille said sweetly. "The deep red stones that Lavinia wears about her neck, were they a gift for spreading her legs?"

Camille was getting into dangerous territory; she knew it by the grim set of his mouth, the tensing of his jaw. Yet, she continued, recklessly. The lies spilled from her mouth before she could stop them. "Lavinia and I are so much alike. We are both whores. Yet for some reason, you shower her with gifts and fancy clothing while you despise me." She moved closer to him, close enough that their lips were nearly touching.

"What happened with Marlena? Was she too proper?"

He looked as if he would strike her. Camille didn't care. She was too angry.

His mouth descended in a fury, his lips slashing across hers, his arms crushing her brutally against him. She struggled but he wouldn't relent; it was a kiss that went far beyond her meager experience; savage, brutal, untamed. She could feel the emotions he'd been holding in check; the angry, hot brand of his mouth on hers. He brought his head up for a mere moment. "If you wished to be treated as a whore, you should've said so."

His lips returned with force, hot, searing, branding her with ruthless possession. There was nothing tender about it; it was raw and powerful and bruising.

She tore her mouth free, gasping for breath. Triumph and challenge glittered in his eyes. Though her throat was burning with the threat of tears, she held her spine rigid then turned and slipped quietly from the room, unaware of how those gold eyes followed the slim sway of her hips, the tender curve of her waist, the sway of blonde curls at her nape.

36

Camille quickly learned that the excuse of a headache was a lady's best friend. She did not dance the first dance with her husband that night, nor did she enjoy seeing the colorful fireworks bursting in the sky, the charades, the games. She retired early to her new chambers, and closed the door.

She lit a candle, for the large room which was now hers was often dim, even in late afternoon. She placed the candle on the bureau and looked at herself in the mirror. She undressed, pulling the combs from her hair, letting the glittering mass fall free about her shoulders. She put her hands on her waist, turning her slender body, silently measuring herself against Lavinia.

She slipped a nightdress over her head, wiggled her hands through the voluminous sleeves. Beneath it she dropped her stays and chemise and stepped out of them. Undoing the pins from her hair, she wrapped the gleaming rope of it around one arm, fastening it in a roll on her neck. "Too thin," she said to her image.

She practically threw herself on the bed and fell asleep for awhile. When she awoke, it was the middle of the night, entirely dark but for the small candle. She thought of the woman claiming to be her grandmother. Should she contact Josephine Huxley? Was it possible her *whole life had been a lie?*

She heard the thud of horses' hooves and crossed to the window. She saw Nicholas below, thundering out of the yard. Was he headed for the coffeehouses? Did he have a townhouse where he kept his mistress? If anyone should understand how it felt to be imprisoned, how a soul longed to be free, it was Nicholas. He was, after all, a man of the sea.

Camille shivered. There was an odd smell in the air. Not just horses and thick grasses, but the smell of tide flats and river. She knew Nicholas wore a pistol and a knife in his belt, wore it with

alarming ease.

37

Two days later, a letter arrived by horseback for Camille. She took it to her room so she could read it in private. Was it from Christopher? Her heart soared with hope. Carefully, she slid a finger under the red seal of wax, breaking it, and began to read.

My dearest Camille,

Where should I start? By now you've seen the gossip columns. I wanted to come to you in person, but I thought perhaps a letter first would be best. There is truth to the gossip columns. Never in a million years would I wish you to find out the truth about your birth

in that way. But I was desperate to find you.

My name is Josephine Huxley. My daughter, your mother, died

years ago. She ran away to marry a man I did not approve of. I never

even knew she was pregnant. I recently hired someone to look into

matters, so I could be sure…it's a long story that I'd rather talk to

you about in person. I am beside myself with joy to know I have a

granddaughter.

When my daughter and her husband were killed in a carriage

accident, you were placed in an orphanage. There was a fire. The

records were lost. Still, the detective would not be deterred. I now

have proof that you are my granddaughter, Victoria Josephine

Huxley. That is your name.

Camille stopped reading for a moment. Her real name was

Victoria? She looked at the elegant script again.

I hope you will come at once after you have read this letter, my

dear. I want to be part of your life. I want to know everything about you. If you do not want to come, I shall try to understand. Of course this must all be a shock to you. I look forward to your reply.

Sincerely,

Josephine Huxley

Camille changed quickly into a cloak of blue velvet and a matching bonnet, tied the wide satin bow beneath her chin, and called for the carriage. The jacket fit her straight shoulders smoothly and hugged her small waist, neatly outlining the full, high curve of her small bosom. Well, if I am not a beauty, at least I am passably attractive, she thought.

She wanted to be presentable when she called on Josephine Huxley. If the woman was truly her grandmother, Camille thought, it would mean she had choices. Maybe even a home other than this one.

She caught her reflection in the mirror before she left. The soft helpless femininity of the gown she wore encased a stubborn and determined spirit. Her color was high in her cheekbones; her eyes sparkled.

38

A fire burned brightly in the hearth on the first floor of

Nicholas' townhouse. A stark, blinding fury had come over him after

Camille had left his study, after she had refused to join the party.

The lilting music around him had all sounded the same, the crush of

faces and voices a blur. He fingered the glass of brandy he now held

tightly in his hand then set it down.

His head ached, his whole body ached, his thoughts were erotic,

betraying him. The woman was getting under his skin; she had

openly defied him. Even Lavinia had never gone that far.

A door slammed and he looked up to see Kipp laying his dark,

expensive cloak on a chair. Kipp liked to keep up with the latest fashions while Nicholas preferred older, more comfortable articles of clothing, things he had molded to his body.

"I say, chap, no one's seen you about for quite some time. Thought maybe the Missus was keeping you entertained in the bedroom."

Nicolas scowled. He jutted out his jaw. "You know it's a marriage in name only," he said.

"Yes, and I think it's killing you old chap."

Kipp filled a glass of brandy and took a swig. "Awful stuff," he said, and put it down. "This is ridiculous, you know."

"What's ridiculous?"

"You. Her. Both pretending not to be attracted to each other! It's so, well, *obvious* to everyone but the two of you."

"I am not attracted to that *twit*." The firelight shone on Nick's thoughtful face.

"I've also heard that the tavern girl turns out to be an heiress," Kipp said. "This is quite a pickle. Her 'uncle' is being investigated for rifling through a good part of the girl's fortune. He's disappeared, gone into the swamps for all we know. Must be some truth to the rumor."

Nicholas snapped his head in Kipp's direction. "Can we please change the subject?"

Kipp sat in a chair, leaning back and watching flames dance in the wide marble hearth. "Sure. What do you want to discuss? The state of dry goods, hardware, food? It's a steady market."

"Sweet Jesus," Nicholas said.

"No? How about the England to Australia run? I hear it's busy and there's always a demand for Chinese silks. And the ship you're thinking of buying?"

Nicholas just grunted.

"Your pardon, captain, but the Chinese vessel? I know she was mishandled and the cargo badly chosen. She's the prime example of what happens when a good ship is supplied with a lacking crew. They were a bad lot of men who were dangerous to the ship's success. You'd have to select the crew personally."

"I intend to."

Kipp looked at him sharply. "That hasn't been done in these parts in a long time—if ever. And good men are harder to find now."

"I know the men I want. They'll work for me."

"You would be taking a big risk to antagonize those who supply crews. Perhaps you could manage it for one voyage—but what happens after that, if men are still scarce?

"Men have more opportunities now—inland shipping; they're going to go west in greater numbers than before. Unless wages aboard ships are raised, it will be difficult to get them and keep them for long voyages.

"There will always be men like me, men who follow the sea," Nick said, thinking of Camille, of the lavender smell of her hair and skin.

"Unless there is something to keep them home, something like a beautiful woman with golden blonde hair and intriguing lips...."

"Bloody hell, shut up already!"

"Am I interrupting something?" a feminine voice crooned from the doorway.

Lavinia filled it with her wide white skirts, tapered upward; the stiff brocade curved, cupping her ample breasts, swept into long tight sleeves that left her creamy shoulders and throat bare. Over her arms she carried the scarlet cloak and her rippling black hair glistened in the light from the fire.

Black and white and scarlet, and cheap looking, Nicholas thought for the first time. The stones in her hair were glass. There were tiny lines of fatigue beneath her grey eyes.

When had he become indifferent to her? *He knew when.* When that blonde-haired waif with green-blue eyes had caught him up in marriage.

"I was just leaving," Kipp said, rising from his chair.

"No you weren't. We have business to discuss."

"OK, I wasn't leaving," Kipp said, sitting back down.

"Nick…I thought maybe we could spend some time together this evening. It's been a long time, you know, since we've had any *fun*." She all but threw her full lips into a pout, tracing a finger over the lush curves of a breast in bold invitation.

Nick wasn't even looking at her. "I'm not in the mood, Lavinia.

245

"You arrogant son of a bitch! Now that you have a little wife, you've suddenly developed morals? This isn't the last you'll see of me!"

She turned on her slippers, slamming the heavy oak door on her way out.

Kipp laughed. "This is more serious than I thought."

Nicholas just growled.

"You know, they say her real name is Victoria."

"Camille, Victoria, she's no different than Marlena," Nicholas growled.

"How can you be so sure?" Kipp asked. "I mean, you hardly know the girl."

Nick's mouth turned down. He was reminded of how Camille had responded to his kisses—with fire, innocence, sensuality. It was baffling. She had told him she was a whore, stood in his very study and taunted him with the knowledge. *And yet he still wanted her.*

"Well, chap, you can deny it all you want, but have you considered that if what the gossip columns say is true, she might leave you, have the marriage annulled?"

Nicholas damned himself for giving in to his fury even as he damned his errant wife for causing it. "Have the carriage brought around, good chap."

39

Home. Could it be?

Camille stepped out of the carriage and looked up at the home with the ornate iron grillwork, the scalloped white corners, the beautifully tended gardens. She wanted to hope, wanted to believe…and yet, she couldn't. Not yet. What did this woman have to gain by claiming she was her granddaughter?

Home, she thought with a pang. She no longer knew where that was. She'd been foisted off on Nicholas, a man who clearly didn't want her, who'd married her simply because of a man's dying wish. A man who didn't play by any rules. A man who was handsomer than he had any right to be.

She thought of him now, his shoulders impossibly wide, the muscles of his arms dark and smooth; his chiseled jaw. Her mind ran wild. His bare chest, the dark curling hair that covered it, disappearing beneath the waistband of his breeches. His cool and unsmiling regard. She climbed the steps and raised a white-gloved hand to knock.

A moment later it was opened so forcefully Camille thought it would be torn from its hinges. She stared at the silver-haired woman, and the silver-haired woman stared back, jaw agape. Then Camille was crushed in the tiny woman's embrace.

40

She pulled Camille quickly into a sun parlor and sat down, patting the cushion beside her. Tears ran freely over the woman's face. She was a handsome, elegantly dressed lady with clear blue-silver eyes.

She pressed Camille's hand warmly. "My God, there can be no doubt, no doubt," she said. She stood, walked over to a desk, and pulled something out. She returned and sat down next to Camille and handed her a miniature portrait.

"You are the spitting image of your mother, Alexandria. The spitting image!"

Camille sucked her breath in. My God, she *did* look like the woman in the portrait. The green eyes. The blonde hair. The same oval face.

She looked at Josephine Huxley, curiosity in her eyes. Her throat felt full of tears.

"I have other proof, my dear, but after all these years, I'm so glad I found you. I called her Alex. Everyone did. That foul man who raised you…in a tavern of all places. He's disappeared but I will find him my dear. He will pay for his lies. He wasn't really your uncle."

"My parents…my father? I had memories…flashing memories from long ago. My uncle…he's not my uncle? He told me they were just the fancies of a poor girl and nothing more." Camille started sobbing and they fell into each other's arms. It was a long time later, when the street lamps burned with oil, that Camille finally understood what had happened, finally knew who she really was. And there was no doubt.

250

41

When she got home…when did she start thinking of Nicholas' mansion as her home?…it was very early in the morning. The house was asleep. She wearily climbed the stairs to her chambers and was thankful no one was about.

She didn't remove her cloak, just started to pack a few things. There wasn't much to pack. Then she quietly descended the stairs. She wished she would have time to say goodbye to Damaris and Arabelle, but for now, she needed to leave, needed to gather her thoughts.

She felt an odd ache in her chest as she set the suitcase in the foyer and quietly rang for the carriage.

"Going somewhere?"

The deep, timbered voice slid from the darkness of the study. Nicholas was standing in the doorway, a scowl on his much too handsome face.

Camille was suddenly not so eager to leave. She didn't know why. Her heart bounded to her throat.

"I'm going…home. The rumors…they are true. My mother…Josephine showed me a picture of her Nicholas, and I look just like her!"

Nicholas was silent. She hadn't meant to use his first name. It just slipped out, intimately.

Silence mounted, thick and heavy. "I think we should discuss this matter further."

"There's nothing to discuss. I've checked into…matters.

If I annul the marriage, you have still fulfilled your obligation and your father's wishes. I understand that you also married me so that you wouldn't lose your family estates." She steadied herself, feeling the ache of sadness spreading throughout her being.

"I don't judge you for that. This has always been your home. I probably would have done the same thing, if I'd had a home like this." Her voice trembled.

"It's funny," she said. "Now that I know who I am...I don't really feel like I know who I am. I do know I am the wife you didn't want. That's the only thing I'm sure of...and I will be happy to free you from this troubling marriage."

She let her eyes rove over his rugged face, the deep dark gold of his eyes, the slant of his brow, the strength of his chin. She remembered the feel of his lips, hot and eager, searching hers. "Goodbye Nicholas," she said abruptly. "I am truly sorry if I caused you any pain." She lifted her small luggage and left him there, in the slanting darkness of the vast hallway. He didn't try to stop her, and she cried all the way to Josephine's...to her grandmother's house.

42

To keep Camille's mind off of matters—she'd sobbed her heart out to Josephine but hadn't gone so far as to say she was in love—Josephine threw parties. Lots of parties. She and Camille had decided it would be best to call her Camille, as that had been her name for most of her life until now.

Josephine proudly introduced her to young men and women and soon, Camille had a small circle of friends. Still, Josephine could see that the terrible ache had not gone from the girl's soul. She was in love with her husband, even if she couldn't yet admit it to herself.

She'd also had another reason for keeping the girl distracted. She'd done some snooping about town, and believed that her husband may have been falling in love with Camille when she left. She had to keep Camille so busy that she wouldn't have time to meet with the lawyer about getting her marriage annulled. Not just yet, she thought. Maybe a little time. Let's see what develops. Josephine chided herself. *Hopeless, old romantic.*

Josephine was keeping herself busy too, if she was honest. Henree had left her employ several weeks after she'd made a fool of herself. She didn't blame him. She didn't want to think about the smile dancing in his eyes, the way she'd felt when she had fallen into his arms, when their lips were so close. Could a woman her age fall in love for the first time? Had he gone to the woman he'd said he'd loved for so long?

She shook herself free of her thoughts and began circling among her guests. It was a beautiful summer evening with the faintest of breezes, and Camille looked lovely in pale green silk, like a ripple of ocean. She even smiled once in a

while. Well, it's a start, Josephine thought.

43

The dance ended. No sooner had it ended then a gentleman she'd never seen before asked her for the next. Wearily, she agreed. He introduced himself and Camille thought for sure she hadn't heard him correctly.

"I'm sorry, I'm feeling a bit flushed this evening from the heat. What did you say your name was?"

"Philip. Philip Branton."

One hand possessively at her waist, Philip led her onto the floor and twirled her around her aunt's ballroom until she was dizzy. "You're my brother's wife. Curious."

Camille felt dizzy.

"I see you're confused. Let me fill you in. I just got back into town. I've been reading the papers. It's a shame you and my brother haven't been getting along." He traced a finger boldly across her collarbone. She stepped away from him. He laughed. He had golden hair, blue eyes, and a pointed chin.

"Really, my dear, no need to be so frosty. Am I not more pleasant to look at than my brother? I can assure you I am much better in the bedroom. At least, his first wife told me so. I meant to surprise my brother at one his lavish parties but this is even better."

Camille was too shocked to reply. Philip chose that moment to look past her and pull her roughly into his embrace. The room went deathly still. Several dowagers grasped. "He's....here!" someone gasped.

Camille pulled away from Philip again, almost slapping him. She took a glass of fizzing champagne from a tray to steady her nerves, unaware of what was transpiring behind her.

"It's him!" someone said.

"Who?" another girl asked.

"Her *husband*."

Camille whirled around. Her heart lurched. She very nearly dropped the glass of champagne.

"He's coming this way," someone whispered. "I wouldn't want to be in *her* slippers right now!"

"He does look rather jealous."

Nicholas bore down on them. Camille felt warm. Judging from the expression on his face, she guessed he wasn't jealous at all. He was merely livid. The anger in his eyes was naked, primitive.

"Camille," he said, his smile devastating, "I see you've made the acquaintance of my brother Philip."

He turned glacial eyes on Philip, eyes that were as cold as frozen bricks of gold. Camille's stomach twisted into a knot. "I wondered when you would show your wretched face again. I'm not surprised you choose this moment."

Philip laughed. "Your wife is lovely. A shame you share separate residences."

The crowd gasped. Nicholas' arm came about Camille's waist, tightening like a cord. He growled. "She's coming home with me tonight, where she belongs."

"Excuse me." Someone tapped on Nicholas shoulder. "I believe Camille promised the next dance to me...."

Nicholas turned. "I'm afraid you're out of luck. As I said, my lovely, enchanting wife is coming home with me."

He turned back to Camille and the red-faced suitor slunk away. Camille's mouth turned down, her lips set in a frown.

"I don't recall promising to come home with you," she said quietly.

"Have you forgotten your wedding vows so soon?" he mocked.

Camille felt furious. How dare he treat her this way in front of her guests! Her grandmother! Why must he always have his way? She wriggled free of his grasp. "I'm not going anywhere tonight."

He smiled, a dazzling flash of white teeth. Then, without another word, he hoisted her over his broad shoulder like a sack of flour.

"Put me down!" she screamed, batting at his back with her small fists.

He strolled across the floor, creating a scandal in his wake. "Dear brother, I'll be calling on you soon," Philip called. Nicholas ignored him.

When they were home, he deposited her on a settee in the parlor and closed the doors. He removed his coat, dropping it onto the back of a chair. He proceeded to undo the top buttons of his shirt.

"What are you doing?"

He'd made no secret of his distaste for her...for what he thought she was.

"Tell me, Camille. Is my brother a charming dancer? Entertaining?"

Her temper flared but she held it in check. She could feel the anger in him.

"Mr. Branton, I hadn't met your brother until a few moments before you so rudely threw me over your shoulder and hauled me out of my grandmother's home. I didn't have time to form an opinion."

"Well, let me form it for you."

"No need," Camille said. "I found him incredibly arrogant, forward, and distasteful. There. Are you satisfied?"

The merest surprise crossed his features. "I thought you said you hadn't formed an opinion. Ah. You must be overly tired. You should go to bed."

"I'm not going to bed here. I'm going home. So please, say what it is you have to say."

Nicholas stood and scratched at his chin, his hair. For the first time in her life, Camille wanted to be treated like a wife…like a woman. A woman desired by this man before her.

He looked tired. She understood again that her husband was a man who would not easily reveal himself. "Have you annulled the marriage?"

"No."

Her smile slipped. Her fingers were icy, clasped in her lap.

"If you would like me to look into it…I could do so tomorrow. I'm afraid my grandmother has kept me insanely busy."

He was silent for a few moments. Gone was the man whose kisses burned her soul, whose arms crushed her in their steely, heated embrace, whose passion overwhelmed her.

"No," he finally said.

"Can you honestly say you want me to stay here, live here, as your wife? That you won't humiliate me, take mistresses out in public view? Is it the money? Because my uncle went through most of it…."

"Camille, I don't know what I want. I…."

"I'll go then," she said quickly. A pang swept through her. She had been hoping for…for what? For the man to love her? Cherish her? Treat her as if he desired her, worshiped her?

Bloody hell yes.

This could not go on. It seemed there was only one choice.

He didn't stop her. She returned to her grandmother's lavish home and paced most of the night in her bedchamber. She felt an unbridled passion, a need so strong she didn't understand it. What was *wrong* with her?

44

Two days later, Meagan sat in the parlor talking with Camille, her dark copper hair curled about her nape and looking lustrous again. Her bruises were nearly healed. She smiled and even laughed once in a while, and Camille felt a great joy to see her, to talk with her, to see she was doing better.

She'd told Meagan everything and Meagan had come to the same conclusion as Josephine. Camille, for all her denials, *felt* something for Nicholas Branton. And though she didn't know it, she was miserable without him.

They sipped soothing tea and nibbled on the delicious tea cakes and ginger nuts her grandmother always had around, afternoon sunshine pouring through the tall laced windows.

"I'm surprised you're not at the lavish party at the Brantons. Especially surprised since Nicholas will be racing against his brother Philip."

"What?" Camille said, dazed. "When?"

The race will probably begin in about an hour or so. It's all over town. You didn't know?"

Camille looked bemused.

"Philip showed up at a party, challenged Nick in front of all the guests. Nick didn't back down."

"Why would Philip want to challenge Nick to a race?"

"Philip, the long lost son returns home after his father dies and finds that Nick's inherited everything. I'd say it was pride. And the winner gets the Branton estates."

"Dear sweet Jesus. Get your jacket, Meagan. We're going to that race."

Meagan smiled to herself. Mission accomplished.

45

"We'll never make it in time if we take the carriage," Camille said. "How do you feel about horses?"

Camille and Meagan were soon riding at a breakneck speed on a horse from Josephine's stables, hooves eating up back roads with fury. Meagan, who'd never been on a horse, held on to Camille for dear life. Secretly, she was thrilled with the adventure they were having.

Camille had an uneasy feeling in her stomach. Something just wasn't right. Yes, Philip was arrogant, vain, spiteful. But something else was wrong. Why did she feel such a sense of urgency?

Nicholas had talked about the races. She'd seen the racing course on the Branton property, close to the main river road in front of the mansion. It was a mile course with curves, and wide enough for horses to pass each other, mud flying off their tremendously thundering hooves.

She was sure people had flocked to the levee, an excellent place to watch, nearest the finish line.

"Hold on," she called back to Meagan as the mansion came into view. "We're taking a short cut. If we go along the river bank, we'll emerge up by the trees, behind the finish line." She could see the colorful, elegantly dressed guests in the distance, people she knew would be betting on the race.

She saw, for the first time, little bands of romantic-looking gypsies. She'd heard they sometimes camped on the levee for the night, selling nostrums and telling fortunes. She also knew that sometimes mansions changed hands on the outcome of a race. *Dear God, Nicholas, no. You don't have to prove anything to anyone! The man's damnable pride!*

She spurred the horse on, and in no time they were up above the track and the finish line and the people. She slowed the horse, knowing they were not visible behind the thick line of oaks. She had no idea what to do next.

"Are you alright?" she asked Meagan.

"Let's do it again!"

Camille laughed, squinting through the tangled arc of branches and leaves and tree trunks. Then she froze. Chills raced over her. "Oh my God," she whispered.

"What? What is it?" Meagan asked.

"Don't talk," she whispered again. "There's a man. A man with a rifle, crouching in those bushes over there. When those horses come down the track, before they get to the finish line….oh my God! We've got to stop him!"

"Hold on!"

Meagan squeezed Camille's waist and closed her eyes for a brief moment as they horse shot out from the brush on a straight line toward the man with the rifle. At the same time, they heard two horses getting closer, thundering down the track. *Please God, please, let me make it to him before Nicholas does!*

Keeping the man in her sights, guiding the horse through the tangle of trees, Camille plunged on. They were far enough away that the man hadn't heard their approach yet.

Nicholas and Philip were neck and neck atop powerfully muscled, sleek quarter horses. With alarm, she realized Nicholas was closest to the man with the rifle, and the man had lifted the horrid gun and was aiming it at Nicholas!

The thundering of the racers crowded out any other sounds. Just as he squeezed the trigger, Camille bounded into the brush, knocking the man and the gun to the ground.

The crowd gasped as Nicholas was flung back, off of his horse.

Kipp and a few other men quickly surrounded Nicholas. The man with the rifle was now lying dazed in the brush.

Camille vaulted off the horse and ran to Nicholas, who was lying unconscious in the middle of the racing lane, blood seeping beneath his white shirt. "My God, Nicholas, no," she breathed as she bent over him.

Soon others were bent over him and while several men apprehended the shooter, Nicholas was carried into the house. In the great commotion, everyone forgot about Philip.

46

The doctor, a man of robust frame, keen and energetic in appearance with remarkably piercing black eyes, quietly closed the door to Nicholas' chamber.

Genevieve and Camille had been waiting in the hall for what seemed like hours for his prognosis. He looked at them levelly. "A few inches more, and it would have been his heart."

Genny nearly collapsed in Camille's arms. "You mean?"

"Yes, he would've died instantly if it wasn't for your bravery, madame."

"Is he going to…be alright?" Camille asked while Genny sobbed.

"I believe he's going to pull through." Tears of relief slid down Camille's cheeks.

Genevieve looked at her in awe. "My God, you saved his life. But how did you know?"

"I didn't. Meagan came to visit and told me about the race shortly before it was supposed to start. I didn't want Nicholas to see me, so I took a back route. I was too late to stop the race and I didn't know what I was going to do but I felt an urgency and acted on it. I saw the man with the rifle," her voice caught, "crouching in the brush. I only did what came naturally."

Nicholas moaned. "Is he awake?" Genny asked the doctor.

"No. He's in a lot of pain. He's lost a lot of blood. Fortunately, the shot hit his arm and not his chest. I've arrested the bleeding, cleaned the wound, and removed the bullet. I've sutured it, so now we'll have to watch for fever. Someone will need to cleanse the wound with carbolic acid lotion."

The question stood in Camille's eyes. Genny blinked, her thick black lashes wet with her tears. "Yes, by all means. You should be the one to do it."

"Thank you," Camille said quietly.

"He'll need a lot of rest," the doctor admonished.

"Thank you Dr. Adams," Genny said. "Thank you so much."

He nodded and left. Camille and Genny quietly entered Nick's room. He slept, his skin pale. Without thinking about it, Camille ran a finger softly over his brow.

They stayed by his side for hours. Genny eventually went to see about the girls, leaving Camille asleep in a chair by Nick's side.

47

Camille stayed by Nick's side for two more nights, nursing

him, cleaning the wound, soothing his jerking body when the lotion

was applied. When she knew for sure he was going to be alright, she

came to a decision. She didn't belong here. She'd caused him

enough grief. Her own feelings, well, she would sort them out later.

She wrote a letter to Genny, explaining how she felt, telling her

she was so sorry to have caused them all heartache. In the middle of

the night, she left the note downstairs, where Genny would be sure to

find it, and left.

When she thought about Nicholas, pain knifed her soul, pain

and longing. Genny had told her that Kipp had hired a detective, and that Philip, under suspicion for arranging the attempted murder, had fled town. Kipp was a good friend to Nicholas. She was glad.

As the carriage carried her back to Josephine's, Camille could barely keep her eyes open. Just before she dozed off she realized, with a start, that she was in love with Nicholas. And it was too late. Too late to do anything about it.

48

Camille passed the next few weeks in abject misery. No amount

of entertaining could raise her out of it, though Josephine tried.

Josephine knew that her granddaughter would have to find her way

on her own, sort out her feelings. And when she did, she would have

to make a decision. She'd even heard rumors that Nicholas' first

wife Marlena was still alive and had been with Philip the whole

time. That she hadn't drowned like everyone believed.

Meanwhile, the steady stream of guests and parties exhausted

Camille. The summer was coming to an end; the nights were clear

and beautiful.

She knew that Nicholas was well healed by now, that he'd come to see her a few times, but she'd refused to come down. She just wasn't ready to face him, and he'd gone away. Finally, he'd stopped calling and Camille felt an emptiness beyond anything reasonable.

Awaking from an afternoon nap to a pleasant breeze coming through the window of her bedroom, Camille was informed she had a visitor. Her heart beat wildly. Nicholas. *How many times can I refuse him?*

She carefully brushed her hair, chose a pale green day dress and matching slippers, and checked her reflection. Her cheeks were once again flushed; her eyes were dark and stormy. She descended the stairs and entered the parlor, only to stop mid-stride.

Josephine rose and came to grasp Camille's arm. "Camille, this fine young gentlemen tells me that you know each other. He's been away at sea for a long time and he wanted to pay you a visit."

Christopher.

He was different somehow. He looked paler and thinner but just as friendly. He stood and gallantly bent low over her hand and kissed it. "Camille, you look fetching as always. There've been a lot of changes in your life. Josephine filled me in."

"Christopher, it's so good to see you. You're looking well."

They sat down together and a servant bustled in with tea, coffee, and cakes.

They talked as the strangers they were and Camille tried to find the feelings she'd once felt for him but couldn't, even when she looked deep down. The only thing she saw were gold-brown eyes, arrogant, laughing at her, mocking her, challenging her, roving over her with desire.

"When did you arrive? Where have you sailed from?"

"I've been many places, most recently China."

"Oh, that's interesting," Camille said.

Christopher scratched his head and Camille noticed his scraggly whiskers for the first time, the hard calluses on his hands. "I have to say, I was surprised to get your letter."

Camille blushed, embarrassed. "You were always so kind to me," she said.

"You didn't have it easy, that's for sure." He smiled, and dimples appeared in his boyish cheeks. Camille couldn't help herself, but she kept comparing him to Nicholas. Christopher still seemed like such a boy, where Nicholas was a *man*.

"I'm not sure how to say this, but I...I can't reciprocate your feelings. I think you're lovely, don't get me wrong, but....but I was married overseas."

Camille felt a flood of relief. She took his hand in hers. "Christopher, it was kind of you to come and see me while you're here. You've come a long way. I hope it hasn't inconvenienced you."

"Nah," he said. "My ship came into port here."

The two sat for an awkward silence.

"Well, but you're right," Camille said. "A lot has changed. I've...I've married too." She didn't want to think about the annulment she would have to get soon.

"Oh?" he said. "Congratulations. I truly hope you're happy."

Camille smiled, not unaware of the sailor's discomfort at being in her grandmother's home, surrounded by frilly, fragile, lacey things. She had to remember he was used to the roughness of the sea.

She hadn't told him she was married in the letter. She was afraid he might not come to see her. But now that he had, she didn't feel the things she'd thought she felt for him.

A short while later, she escorted him out, wishing him all the happiness in the world. Then she remembered she had to get dressed for dinner and dancing, again. It was the last thing she felt like doing.

49

Camille was dressed in a gold gown with black piping; the fabric was light with a high waistline and short puffed sleeves. The Italian opera season was coming to an end and Camille wished she were outside, drinking deep of the cool evening air, instead of within a crush of faces. She was glad the summer was coming to an end and that the fresh, crisp fall days would soon be here. Men and women had arrived at Josephine's house after having dined at the home of Alice Mercury, and they would meet Alice and others of her party again at the Opera House.

Camille sighed, needing to escape to the gardens. When the musicians took a break for refreshments, she slipped outside, into the cool, dark night that whispered with brilliant stars. A glow in the eastern horizon gave promise of a full moon.

She sat for a while on a marble bench, her eyes closed, the breeze caressing her, easing the thin sheen of perspiration from her neck.

"You've avoided me for far too long."

She opened her eyes to find Nicholas standing before her, elegantly attired in a black jacket, crisp white shirt and black trousers.

Camille trembled slightly. "How…how is your arm?" she asked quietly.

"The bone aches, down to my very being, but I'm alive." His eyes pierced hers. "Thanks to you."

She stood, uncertain of her feelings, of what to say or do. He solved her dilemma by pulling her into his embrace, his dark good looks reaching into her very womb. She closed her eyes. She knew she would be lost if she looked at him.

"Open your eyes, my sweet. There are things I need to say…but not with words."

Before she could utter a reply, his lips descended on hers. It wasn't with the savage brutality she expected, but with a thorough, seductive gentleness.

Her heart hammered. She splayed her fingers on his hard, muscular chest, letting all her pent up feelings go, letting him have his way, letting him lead her with his lips.

"Why…did you come?" she finally breathed. In answer, he swept her into his arms and carried her to an alcove, a private gazebo festooned—actually nearly covered—with roses and vines. He sat on the bench and positioned her intimately on his lap. "You're my wife. A man has a right to call on his wife."

He hiked up her skirt. The feel of his hand on her thigh, rolling down her stockings, was a heated shock. A strange feeling swirled in the pit of her stomach; ravenous warmth began to eat at her soul. "What are you doing?"

"What I should have done long ago, my sweet. Breaking my vow. Ending the sham. Thoughts of you have been driving me crazy. It's time I did something about it."

His hand left her thigh for only a moment to remove her shoes. Deftly, he rolled her stockings down and discarded them on the floor of the gazebo, amid the scattered petals of apricot and pink roses.

His bold, searching hand moved even higher on her thigh. Camille was frightened. "Don't…please! If you touch me again, I'll burst into flames!"

Laughter rumbled in his chest. "You do realize that's a compliment, my sweet, don't you?"

He crushed her in his embrace once more, his kisses igniting a fire within her that threatened to consume them both. He forced her lips apart, his tongue delving into the honeyed interior of her mouth, searching, beseeching, claiming. She felt the roughness of his five o'clock shadow against her skin. Her breathing gone ragged, her mind gone blank and replaced with a hazy spiral of passion that threatened to blaze headily out of control, she reached up, twining her slender fingers into his thick dark hair. Sweet God, but she had wanted to do that for so long. It no longer mattered that he was who he was. That she was who she was. That they were completely unsuited. He was her lawfully wedded husband, and she was his wife.

"Tell me what you want Camille." There was unmistakable male victory in his voice.

"I…don't know...I want…your hands on me. I want to … touch you."

She waited, afraid he would change his mind, afraid he'd come here to simply thank her for saving his life and that he would agree to an annulment, that with a signing of a paper, she could end it all and he would walk away, back to Lavinia.

In that instant, she bared her soul to him. She held her breath as heated gold-brown eyes delved into hers.

His voice was gruff. "Say my name. I want to hear it on your lips. I want to be sure." His breath was on her ear. "Because once I start, my dear, there will be no turning back. Tell me you understand this."

Camille nodded. Her tongue darted out to lick her rosebud lips. He watched the movement like a hawk watches his prey.

"Nick…Nicholas…touch me…please. I…want to know your touch."

286

He made a sound. A husky growl.

Her voice was a thin silky whisper that set his blood afire, his loins to near bursting. "This night, you will belong to me. I will make you mine. Do you understand?" Her veins pulsing with pleasure, her mind numbed to thought, she nodded weakly.

Vaguely, it puzzled Nick that she seemed so innocent and was even now trembling in his arms. He knew she was not innocent of men, and yet there was something virginal about her acquiescence. Though he longed for nothing more than to bury his shaft deep within her womanly core, he held himself back.

"Touch me, feel me, know how I desire you." He took her small hand and placed it on his manhood, which was thick and swollen with need, straining to break free of his trousers. Camille gasped—remembering how large, how thick, he was. His lips came back to her neck. She pulled her hand away. "Now is not the time for modesty, my dear.

"I won't hurt you. I can't promise I'll be gentle; I've wanted you for far too long. But I won't hurt you. Never would I hurt you."

He undid his trousers. He was thick with need of her.

She watched in wonder as he slipped them down with his other hand, staring at that manly part of him that was so foreign to her. Sweet God, but she did not know how to touch a man. He took her hand, placed it on his shaft. It was like holding velvet fire.

His heat branded her, sending jagged, silver sparks of desire coursing throughout her body. He groaned, staring as her slender fingers wrapped themselves around him intimately. He shuddered. At the same moment, he eased her thighs apart with his hand and began stroking the most intimate, womanly part of her—the part that held her sweet secrets.

He stroked and cajoled and manipulated her womanly flesh, then delved a finger into her molten heat. Camille gasped. Ragged, savage eddies of pleasure swirled through her being; fires of passion sizzled in her soul. Instinctively, her fingers began to move, tentatively at first, then feverishly in tandem with his finger, which plunged in and out of her, creating a need within her that she didn't fully understand.

She arched her back in pleasure, opening her legs wider to him.

"My God, Camille, you are so sensual. I'm going to pleasure you as you've never been pleasured before."

As you've never been pleasured before.

His words barely penetrated the haze of passion. But penetrate they did. She hated herself in that small moment, hated how easily she lost herself to him. One glance, one touch from this man who had promised never to want her, and she melted.

"What do you mean?" she said, barely able to speak.

"Come now. You act so innocent. There is no need."

Her voice was but a tremor. "You…You still think me a common whore who only plays the innocent?"

"The past is the past. I care not that…there were others before me."

"I was a fool to think you could desire me. You came here to hurt me. You said it before—you had no desire to sleep with a common tavern maid."

Tears threatened to spill down her cheeks and a great ache arose in her throat. "What is it? Now that you know I'm not related to

Penley you will deign to sleep with me? Because I'm a little less tarnished? Is that it?

"Is this a game for you? I cannot…*will* not give myself to a man who thinks his wife a common whore. Not matter how much I l…." She stopped herself before she said it. *Love you.*

He laughed, a hard-edged sound that knocked against the night. His arms came about her, hard bands of corded steel muscle, mercilessly crushing her to him. "You cannot stop this now, my sweet. It is far too late for that."

Nicholas was angry, angry that she could turn her desire on and off like that, that she could push him away; whereas he felt he would surely die if he did not feel himself buried to the hilt inside of her. Why didn't she desire him as she did other men? Men like the red-bearded sailor in the tavern? The thought made him suddenly angry.

He pushed her down against the wooden bench. "I'm sorry it has to be this way, love," he rasped, "for I wanted to savor you. I wanted to show you how it could be different. I'm not like those other men; God only knows how many there have been before me.

But it's too late. You've pushed me beyond what any man can endure. I want you beyond all reason. I have to have you. *Now*."

His lips crashed down on her mouth as his hands deftly bared her creamy shoulder. He nipped it gently before renting her dress off her shoulders, exposing an erect, coral-tipped nipple to the night…and to his hand.

His voice was husky. "You can deny me all you want with words, but your body betrays your needs...needs I will satisfy this night."

Roughly, his hand came up to palm her breast, squeezing and kneading the small mound. Camille watched in wonder the long, dark fingers splayed across her white, tender flesh, barely able to breath. She moaned despite herself. "Nicholas, no…" Her plea was pitiful and he knew it.

It was true; she did want him. Her body was a pliant traitor, seeking only pleasure at his hands. All rational thought fell away when he touched her, when he raked her with his eyes. She remembered the wondrous waves of heat he'd created in her body that night in the study. Could it happen again? Would it always happen with him?

He hiked her skirts higher, admiring the slim, womanly curves of her hips, his fingers stroking and plunging into her, making her frenzied.

She moaned, closed her eyes, feeling hot with shame, and yet she did not want him to stop.

"You are wet with need of me," he breathed. His voice was low, male, utterly possessive. "Now I make you wife truly." His thigh nudged her legs further apart and with a start, Camille realized the hot tip of his manhood was positioned between her legs, poised and ready to plunge within her heated, satin walls.

She was slick in response to the ministrations of his masculine fingers. She made the mistake of meeting his eyes, blonde with heat. "Let me in, Camille. Touch my cock, feel us there together."

She would not grant him acceptance with words nor would she deny him. She was lost once more to his passion. He did not move, but his fingers, sweet God, his fingers began to ply her flesh once more, the hot manly tip of him still at her entrance. She threw her head back in pleasure as he easily wrought in her what he was seeking—a hot shard of pleasure spasmed through her body, aching and sweet, spreading out across her very being, pulsing and vibrating against his fingers. Her hand caressed the tip of him, the, long hard shaft at the same time. Her limbs weak and quaking with pleasure, Nicholas did not wait. He needed no further invitation.

He rammed himself inside her, hard to her woman's core, then went utterly still. Camille cried out in pain, feeling the fullness of him, feeling as if she'd been rent in two, passion replaced by pain. She gasped in pain. Vaguely she thought Meagan was right. It's the man who finds pleasure, the woman who finds pain.

Nicholas couldn't believe it—she was a virgin! Damn, a virgin! Why hadn't she told him? A hot current of anger and shame swept through him, for she'd never denied his accusations. He realized belatedly that she was too proud for that.

"Damn me, but you should have told me you were a virgin." Again he was incredulous. She had never refuted his accusations, never denied them. *Not once.* Why had she let him believe she was a whore, a woman experienced of men when she had never been touched *by any other* except him? The fact that he was the first gave him an odd pleasure, mingling with guilt, lending an odd ache to his breast, making him even harder. He wished he could be more gentle, but he'd wanted her so badly.

The hot tightness of her virginal walls, the upward thrust of her small rounded breasts, her quivering nipples erect with need—all of it was too much for him, even for a man of his experience.

His fingers took hold of her shoulders firmly. He hated himself for his weakness for her. She could so easily make him want her, more than any woman he'd ever wanted. "There is no help for it," he groaned. "Please, I cannot…stop…." He plunged inside her, over and over. She moaned and then he spilled his hot seed within her. He could not hold back.

He nuzzled her neck quietly for a few moments. She'd gone utterly still. He pulled away from her then, sitting up, spent and frustrated and angry. He pulled his trousers back into place.

"It didn't have to be like this, Camille. The next time…"

Camille, sobbing now, sat up, the sound renting his breast.

"Next time? There won't be a next time, Nicholas!" She turned away from him, clutching her torn dress about her.

"Camille, I could have given you even more pleasure…if only I'd known…"

"It's a lie! Only the man finds pleasure. I was told, but I never believed it…until now. I…I hate you!" she cried. "The only thing you've ever given me is pain! You made up your mind about me from the first moment you saw me—and you never saw any other side of me!

"And you broke your promise," she said hoarsely. *"You broke your promise!"*

Nicholas was silent for a long moment, watching her small shoulders shake as she sobbed. He wanted to reach out to her, touch her, soothe her, tell her it would be alright. Damn, but he'd screwed this up royally. Maybe even lost her forever. He felt a bleak emptiness well up in his soul, an unexplainable blackness. He reached out to touch her, then thought better of it.

His voice was a whisper, tinged with regret. "You will be sore in the morning. A warm bath should ease the ache."

"If only a warm bath could wash away this entire night...wash away the thought of you ever touching me!"

In the darkness, with her back to him, she did not see the hard frown that crossed his features.

"Damn me, Camille, but I never meant to hurt you! You aren't blameless, you know. You wanted this as much as I did. Tell me you didn't."

She could not.

She heard him finish dressing then storm away, his heavy booted footfalls taking him quickly down the path to the street, where his carriage no doubt waited. Where would he go? Camille wondered if he would spend the night in Lavinia's bed. She seemed to enjoy the lovemaking between a man and a woman, perhaps even satisfied Nicholas in a way that she, inexperienced in these matters, could not.

A strange coldness crept into her heart. She sat up, alone in the gazebo except for the scattered rose petals. Her fingers curled deeper into the rend of her dress. There was a stinging numbness between her legs. She remembered the feel of him there and a heated throbbing began again. No, damn him! None of it made any sense!

He was a devil, practiced at seduction. He'd taken everything she'

ever had to give. And he'd broken his word. Damn him, he'd broken

his word!

It was late. Camille cursed Nicholas again, gathered herself up,

and quietly made her way into the house and up the stairs to her

bedchamber, careful not to awaken anyone. She was not sure of the

hour, but she knew that dawn would soon creep traitorously over the

horizon as if the night had never been.

Angrily, she grasped the pitcher from her bedside table, filled

the basin with water, and dipped a cloth into the water. She placed it

gingerly between her legs. It was a cool shock, but not as shocking

as the slight sheen of blood on her thighs, illuminated by a sliver of

copper moonlight slipping through the window.

She wiped her thighs more vigorously. How did women endure

such pain in the marriage bed night after night?

Oh how she longed for that bath! The sooner she had it, the

sooner she could wash away the lingering male scent of her husband,

297

the feel of the man who'd taken her innocence, found pleasure, and

left her only pain.

50

Camille and Genny walked the wharves, enjoying the bright sun glinting off the impressive ships. Goods were piled everywhere; bales of cotton, stacks of lumber, barrels of sugar. Stevedores and laborers worked among traders and brokers. Street vendors raised their voices in an odd chorus, trying to sell their various goods. Mules and dray horses drew all sorts of vehicles as visitors disembarked from riverboats and ships.

Camille had invited Genny to go for a walk before having dinner at Josephine's. There were things she wanted to say to her, and didn't quite know how.

"How are the girls doing? I miss them."

"They miss you too," Genny replied. "And so do I as a matter of fact."

"Everything has been so strange. I'm still trying to make sense of it."

Genny smiled knowingly. "Do you love my brother?"

Camille was silent for a moment. "You don't beat about the bush, do you?"

"That's why you wanted to talk to me, isn't it?"

"You're very perceptive."

"You still haven't answered my question."

"And very persistent."

Camille admired the ships shining in perfect cleanliness, polish, and repair, the brass work sparkling triumphantly. She caught her breath at the size and nearness of them, their bare spars towering high into the sky, thick and sharp, endless and powerful, like the men who commanded them and the men who shouted and swung hammers and mallets.

"The man's as stubborn as a jackass," Genevieve said. "But I can tell you I think he is absolutely, irreversibly, undeniably in love with you."

"What in the world would make you form such an opinion?"

"Because he's miserable too, and he's making everyone else miserable."

"Tell me something Genny. Is your brother made of iron and stone? Because I've often wondered."

Genny laughed. "He doesn't let anyone stand in the way of what he wants, that's for sure."

"Have they found Philip?"

She shook her head. "I think if he comes back, he knows people will blame him for the shooting and he'll be investigated. Who else would go to such lengths to hurt him? Besides, once he found out he didn't stand to inherit anything despite Caindale not being Nicholas' natural father, what point was there in staying?"

"What?"

"Caindale always knew that Nicholas wasn't his son, apparently. It's a shock to the rest of us. Including Nick. Caindale's wife, my mother, had an affair and Nicholas was the result. Why he raised him is a mystery to us all, but I think it's because he always knew deep down that his own son Philip would disappoint him greatly. And because he truly loved his wife despite her indiscretion and would do anything for her.

"Nicholas has had so much heartache and deception in his life," Camille said quietly.

"There's something else I have to tell you. When Philip disappeared, Marlena resurfaced."

Camille stopped and turned toward Genny. "His first wife? So the rumors are true. She's alive. She never drowned and yet made Nicholas feel guilty all this time for her death …."

"Yes. It's been determined that she ran off with Philip long ago and they lived on an island for a while. When they came across a newspaper article about Nick's engagement, well, they made plans. She'd made some appearances around town. Word on the street was that she wanted to stir up trouble for Nicholas. She tried to tell everybody that the annulment of Nick's marriage to her was illegal. He made it years after she disappeared."

Camille bit her lower lip. "How do you know all this?"

Genny smiled wickedly. "I simply asked her. And told her what I would do to her if she ever set foot on our property again."

"She's not right, about the annulment being illegal, is she?"

"Bloody hell no," Genny said. "Nick's a smart one. Don't worry. She has no claim to anything. Ironically, faking her own death assured that."

"My God, the girls. They must be so confused, they must be hurting. Has she been to see them yet? And where has she been all this time?"

"No, thank God. I think the girls don't know yet. And I don't know where she's been. Nick's got someone on it, if I know Nick."

"Well, that's a small miracle."

"Yes it is, as Marlena cares only for herself. I never liked her. She's a gold digger. She always wanted to be wealthier than she was before she married Nick, and she wasn't faithful to him. I found out after she disappeared. Of course, the newspapers made Nick out be some sort of ogre, even insinuated that he'd murdered her."

"How awful for him," Camille said. "Genny, has any woman ever broken her heart trying to influence this man, beating against that rock-like determination of his? Can any flesh and blood woman break him down? Would he ever give up anything of his to bring happiness to another?"

"Some women have tried. Lavinia, God, she's a piece of trash. I hate to sound so crass, but all she wants is attention, money, flattery."

They started walking again, ignoring the cat calls from sailors. "I think you could be that woman," Genevieve said. "I think you *are* that woman."

"I don't know. I love him, and I hate him too. I feel so confused. For what he's done to me. How can that be?"

"That's love I guess. Listen Camille, once Marlena finds out she has no claim to Nick's riches, she'll be gone. I'm sure of it. She'll be on to her next challenge, finding some other man to dupe with her wiles. In the meantime, detectives will dodge her and Philip's every move until they are where they belong—in jail.

"I'm not asking you to make a decision now, but please, think about your feelings. Don't give up on Nick yet. I think he's planning a long sea voyage, and I hate to see him go. I can see him hardening himself to his feelings again. But the right woman could make him stick around."

51

It's not fair, Camille thought. *I can't stop loving him any more than I can stop the motion of the sea.*

But I can do something about it. It had been two weeks since she'd talked with Genny. She'd also heard that when Marlena made a spectacle of herself at the mansion, and when she couldn't legally do anything about her annulled marriage to Nick, that she'd left town, just as Genny had predicted. Hadn't even bothered to inquire about her *own* children. Camille's heart ached for them. That was something else that had made up her mind. The girls needed her, and she needed them.

She didn't bother to change out of her riding habit. There was no time to lose.

52

Camille ran to the stables first, but Nicholas was nowhere to be found. From there she raced up the front steps of the porch to the great hall and finally to the great room, where couples swirled dizzily and laughed enticingly beneath the warm, enchanting glow of candles or sat close together as they sampled gourmet foods on crested English silver. The whole time she heard a voice in her head, *you shouldn't have come back. You don't belong here; you don't belong to him.* But she had to come, she had to find him. She had to tell him what was in her heart, no matter the risk, no matter the cost.

Genny was right. At last she glimpsed him briefly in the velvety throng of dancers.

"Nicholas!"

The crowd gasped and parted for her, a blonde-haired waif in mud-spattered riding breeches and a white shirt, a spot of raucous dirt amidst sparkling young jewels shining in their taffeta, satins, and silks.

"Nicholas!" she called again, for he apparently hadn't heard her. Voices began to whisper as heads turned in her direction. In fact, it seemed everyone had heard her cry, everyone except Nicholas.

He was waltzing with a woman…his head bent low over her ear. Camille felt the breath leave her body in a sickening rush. Lavinia smiled up at him as his finger lazily traced her bare shoulder then tangled in her glossy black hair.

The silence was absolute now, and terrifying. Everyone had drawn back and Camille stood alone, Nicholas only a few feet from her. If she reached out, she could touch him….

He was still unaware of her. Lavinia turned her moon-like eyes on Camille and smiled—a lush, insolate smile.

"Nicholas, please," Camille beseeched. Her voice was the merest of whispers, and very close to begging.

"Why Nicholas, it's your wife. Don't be rude. Talk to her, darling. We'll have time tonight for serious indulgences."

He turned his dark head, his hand still resting much too intimately on Lavinia's creamy shoulder. His chin hardened, like the rest of him, Camille thought.

She spoke fast, the words tumbling out of her. "There's something I have to tell you…something important…."

"My lady, if you'll excuse me, I'm busy at the moment." His tawny eyes burned with anger, perhaps even impatience? Camille wasn't sure. He turned his back to her and Camille felt the world tilt dangerously as he leaned lower and placed a kiss on Lavinia's bare skin.

Camille's voice was a bare canvas in the colorful air between them. "It's not important after all."

She wasn't sure Nicholas heard her now, and she no longer cared. The sadness, the shock and humiliation she felt, was an overpowering ache in her chest. Why was Nicholas treating her this way? She had told him she'd hated him. Perhaps he'd had enough. Perhaps, as Genevieve had said, he'd started returning to the hard man he'd been before she'd met him.

Everyone watched with amusement, pity, and some with glee as she quickly fled the great room.

She'd been the veriest fool. She shouldn't have come. Nicholas was through with her. And he would never know the truth. He would never know what was in her heart.

Tears streamed wildly down her cheeks as she ran from the house, ran blindly into the night, the thought of his hands and his lips on that woman burning in her mind, killing every dream she had ever had. *This is what it feels like to love*, she thought. *Never again.*

Camille didn't see the hand raised in the shadows, didn't have much time to feel the swift, sharp blow that rendered her unconscious as she ran by the ancient boxwood hedges enclosing the lawn.

53

Something unfamiliar touched Camille's eyelids, her nose, her cheeks. *Warm daylight.* She opened her eyes and immediately shut them. Her head throbbed painfully. What happened? Where was she?

Her mouth was dry, her mind sluggish. She tried to sit up, but the movement was too much and she sank back down in a bed. Her head ached and throbbed terribly.

"'Bout time ye woke up," a gruff voice said from the shadows of the room.

Camille opened her eyes despite the pain. She was in a tiny, seemingly airless room with a single window. She heard the sounds of water nearby, of horses and carts in the broken streets below. She could not see who had spoken. The ragged shutters on the window were nearly falling off; she lay on a makeshift bed with a tattered woolen blanket. It was the only piece of furniture in the room. She realized with a start that her hands were tied to the bed posts. She wore only a nightdress.

"Who are you? Where am I and what do you want with me?"

A deep, dark laugh unfurled from the beefy chest of a man who had stepped a little further into the light. *My God, Meletios.*

He stepped fully into the light and grinned mercilessly. "I never did get to beat ye, but at least I had the joy of knocking ye cold."

Camille trembled. She couldn't speak.

"Perhaps I'll beat ye now." He cracked his knuckles, a sound like bone splintering, and took a step toward her.

"Not just yet, Meletios." Camille's "uncle" stepped from the shadows.

"Untie me!"

"My dear, sweet niece. You aren't in a position to make demands. Haven't you figured it out yet? I thought perhaps you had, as you went running back to Nicholas. You must have told him the truth about me."

Camille pulled on the ropes binding her, struggling to no avail as it all came back to her. "You're not my uncle. Everybody knows how you lied to me all those years. I…."

Her uncle looked surprised. "This is even better than I thought." His eyes, like puddles of chimney soot, narrowed as he sat on the edge of the bed, much too close for comfort. He raised a gnarled finger to her cheek.

"I might as well tell you all of it. I really enjoyed living off your inheritance. It was all so easy. No one ever questioned me about the family, about whether I was truly your uncle. It was so easy to take you from the orphanage, once I read the article about your parents' deaths. No one had put two and two together. I checked the orphanages and sure enough, found you. Unclaimed. All that wealth just sitting there. I couldn't let that happen, my dear."

314

"You're disgusting! You lied to me, you made me work in a tavern, you tried to make me think I was crazy for remembering my parents, my home!"

"Of no account now, my dear. Of no account now."

He stood and walked to the window. "Not only are you my prisoner, but no one knows where you are. And more importantly, no one cares! Apparently not even your dear Nicholas. Disposing of you shall be too easy."

"Dis...disposing of me?"

"Yes, my dear. You don't think I can allow you to live, knowing what you know, do you? I don't fare well in prisons and have no desire to return to one."

"But...."

"Do you think your precious Nicholas will come for you? I doubt it. The rumor is, shortly after you left Legacy Oaks he was seen sauntering about town with his lovely black-haired mistress clinging to his arm, you know, the one who willing spreads her legs for him whenever he asks?"

"You won't get away with this."

"Oh? And who's to stop me?" He frowned. "I've wasted enough time on you, my dear." He turned his small, round form toward Meletios. "Go ahead, give her the beating; I know you want to." He looked at Camille. "Goodbye, my dear."

As he opened the door he called back to her. "By the way, screaming won't do you any good. We're in a part of town where screams are commonplace. No one bats an eyelash my dear." Then he was gone and Camille was left staring wide-eyed at Meletios. She screamed anyway.

She pushed herself as far back into the bed as she could without cutting off the circulation in her wrists. Her last conscious thought was of Nicholas. Despite all, she loved him. Her lips tried to form his name but they were too swollen and bloodied by the time Meletios was through to speak it.

54

Nicholas felt something was wrong, terribly, horribly wrong. He gave orders to have his ship turned about and as he sat at night looking over his log he found himself listening, tensely, for any change in the force or direction of the wind, waiting, feeling with every nerve any new motion or sound of the ship.

There was no snuggling down for the night under reduced sail for Nicholas; his ship sped on, and as he logged the miles, he prayed for continued good winds. Angel, his second in command, a big beefy man whose smile revealed several gold teeth, watched him, a smile now and then cracking his broad face. "Aye, the speed of the

Lucinda is more due to her captain than to her hull and rigging. She responds to you like a woman would."

During the day Nicholas kept a glass glued to his eye, and now and then he sighted a sail. He watched for the flags of Britain. The crew thought they were setting a record, but no one talked in the forecastle of it, as the men grabbed every precious spare moment for rest, anxious to keep up with their sleepless, decidedly insane commander.

They sighted a British ship, riding out a gale, but she disappeared quickly in Lucinda's foaming wake.

When he was once again on dry land, he felt like he'd been away for years even though it had only been a little over a week. And the way he'd behaved, the way Camille had appeared, breathless, her voice quiet and desperate in front of all those guests, and then his horrible behavior, trying to make her jealous, how she'd run out of there...it twisted at his gut. Why had he been so hard to her? *He knew the reason.*

He'd learned that Josephine mistakenly believed that Camille had been staying at the plantation while he'd been away. Back on land, Nicholas told her everything and soon, between Nick, Kipp, Josephine, and Genny, they were questioning the servants of the mansion, the stable hands for information, then canvassing the city. The trail turned cold in a rundown part of the city where houses were covered in chimney soot.

A place that pious ministers often referred to as Sodom at the River's Mouth, New Orleans was a city that had first been French, then Spanish, and now Creole, a blending of both. Luxurious and gay; hostile yet welcoming. The Creoles had started coming around to the Americans who had so recently come down the Mississippi to save the city from the British.

The Battle of New Orleans had cemented that friendship and now Americans were welcomed nearly everywhere. But not all pockets of the city were so friendly. Nicholas shivered despite the fact that he was sweating.

It was Sunday, feast day. The Creole population had gone to mass in the morning. Many would attend a cock-fight in the afternoon and a ball in the evening. Saloons would be overflowing with people seeking pleasure. The streets were filled with

Frenchmen, Spaniards, Creoles, and Kentuckians in blue homespun, their pockets stuffed with dollars they'd earned by their long trip down the river. Negro slaves walked barefoot through the streets.

Where was Camille? He had to find her. He'd hurt her. Made her want to curl up inside herself. Guard against everybody. He knew what it was like to feel that way. He'd been selfish and obnoxious because ... he was afraid of the way she made him feel. Afraid of love. He'd been hurt before.

They hadn't been able to find Penley. Nicholas had men fanned out over the entire city looking for Camille, asking questions.

Kipp, Josephine, and Genny headed in one direction and Nicholas in another, basically because the man was so frenzied no one could keep up with him. Up ahead, he could see that the Cathedral was filled with a crowd. Vendors in booths along the iron railings sold oranges, bananas, and ginger beer. Negro women balanced baskets on their heads and cried out their wares. At other stalls, men and women ate oysters fresh from the shell.

Inside the square, quadroon girls wearing bright striped tignons were chaperoned by their mothers, who hoped to snag husbands for their daughters from the well-to-do gentlemen of the town. Nuns in black robes and veils passed, their eyes lowered.

Nicholas felt claustrophobic. He'd never been more afraid. He had to find Camille. Guilt and fear formed a physical weight that pressed on his chest.

And then, a small miracle. Near the Café des Refuigies, a famous coffee house near the market between Dumaine and Saint Philip streets, he spotted him. *Meletios.* Onlookers sat under orange trees, sipping their sweet drinks.

Nicholas picked up his pace and began to follow Meletios. He'd never met the man in person but had uncovered enough information about him and his unique appearance to know it was him. He stood taller than most men, was a solid wall of muscle, had a telltale scar that ran in a jagged line down his right cheek.

A solid, well-muscled arm blocked his progress and Nicholas nearly exploded.

"Easy mate," Henree said. "I'm here to help. I'm Josephine's…well I used to be her butler. She told me about Camille. I'm here to help."

The man appeared to be in his fifties and in very good shape. Nicholas gave him the benefit of the doubt that he was who he said he was.

"Come along then, no time to lose. That man there," Nicholas pointed him out, "is going to be sorry he was ever born by the time I get through with him."

Nicholas and Henree made their way stealthily through the crowd of mostly men, some of whom were busy throwing their last picayunes at the bare feet of exotic Spanish dancers.

Just next door was the Hotel de la Marine, a favorite rendezvous of pirates and gamblers like Jean Lafitte, who had on occasion been seen lounging in the sitting room or drinking next door at the café. The hotel, Nicholas knew, was managed by a frenetic Creole gentleman who gave elaborate entertainments—jugglers and knife throwers often performed along with the dancers.

Meletios had come from the direction of the hotel. Nicholas and Henree followed the rawboned Greek man, who was at least a head taller than both of them.

Nicholas hoped Meletios, who peeled and ate oranges as he walked, dropping the peels on the ground, would lead them to Camille.

The sky was cloudless, the heat oppressive as they followed at a discreet distance, winding down back alleys, deeper into the city of sin.

They were not disappointed when Meletios eventually stopped before a house that looked like it was nearly falling down. It had two floors, the roof a dull blue slate and the walls dull red brick. Solid green wooden shutters hung at crooked angles from the windows. Nicholas could see no movement inside the square glass panes.

The Greek gave a quick turn of his square head, left then right, before his bulky body disappeared inside.

"Do you have any weapons?" Nicholas asked quietly.

"My fists," Henree said. "Used to be a boxer. I still practice."

"Good. I have a pistol and a knife but I'd get more satisfaction from using my fists." Henree nodded.

"A little extra protection is never a bad idea."

"Do you have a preference?" Nicholas asked. Henree shook his head no so Nicholas kept the pistol and handed Henree the knife, which he slid inside his boot.

They waited a few minutes—which seemed like the longest of Nicholas' life and during which they could hear nothing from inside—before they quietly entered the house and climbed a steep and narrow flight of stairs.

55

They were on the second floor. Down the hall they heard a door shut. They crept along until they stood outside it. They waited. Listened. It took every ounce of restraint Nicholas had not to knock that door down and pound Meletios into dust. He looked at Henree. Henree nodded.

The door exploded inward and a surprised Meletios, bent with his fist over someone on the bed, looked up. He smiled wickedly, straightened his spine and Nicholas' heart almost stopped. Camille lay on the bed, sweat plastering a nightgown to her body. Her eyes were closed, her hair mussed, her face bloodied and bruised.

Though white hot anger raged in his chest, an anger that threatened to destroy all in its path, Nicholas hadn't missed the fact that Meletios held a knife in his other hand.

Nicholas had heard the rumor that Meletios once had a girlfriend who betrayed him with another man. The man ended up on the bottom of the Mississippi and Meletios cut off the girlfriend's upper lip and an ear to teach her a lesson.

"Move away from her," Nicholas growled, aware of the weight of the pistol in his coat pocket. He was a pretty good judge of men and he would wager Meletios was a proud man. He'd guessed right.

Meletios laughed—a big, booming sound in the nearly airless room. He was even uglier up close. Had a rheumy film over one eye. His other eye glittered with hate, probably one of the only emotions he was capable of conjuring.

"Two against one? Well, no matter. I will kill you both. With my bare hands. I'm good at that sort of thing." He placed the heavy, wicked-looking blade on a table next to the bed.

Camille still hadn't stirred.

Meletios charged.

The men tangled brutally, savagely, relentlessly. Punches landed with smacks and thuds. Blood spurted. Bone cracked. In his rage, Nicholas saw nothing before him but the man who had harmed Camille. Pain bloomed when Meletios fist connected with his upper right cheek and jaw but he stayed upright.

Henree was light on his feet and surprisingly strong.

Finally Nicholas' fist found its mark, plowing into Meletios brick-like jaw at the same time Henree landed a solid punch to the huge man's gut. Like a snorting mammoth, Meletios spit broken teeth into his palm, dropped them to the floor. Smiled through the blood.

Nicholas' left eye was nearly swollen shut now from a connection with Meletios' meaty fist. Henree rushed into his man, hitting left and right, but receiving heavy jobs in return. Henree's mouth was a river of blood but the chap was still smiling. Cut and battered, he kept going. He boxed low, his right hand drawn across his body to block punches.

Nicholas landed a heavy blow to Meletios' shoulder, dislocating it, but the truth was they didn't have time for this. Nicholas was letting pride get in the way of helping Camille. He didn't know the extent of her injuries. He was wasting time. About to pull his pistol from his pocket and be done with it, he heard a feminine voice.

"Oh bloody hell."

There was an odd thudding sound. Meletios froze mid-punch with an odd look twisting his face. He fell over, a knife jutting from his wide back, blood spilling on the floor.

Camille sat up in the bed now, apparently having woken, cut her bindings lose while the men were fighting, and thrown the knife dead center into Meletios' back. Then she fainted.

56

Camille felt like she was underwater. Tumbling, being carried along in a turbulent current, bumping, twisting, seeing a bright light high in the sky.

She awoke in Nicholas' bed. Nicholas, his face swollen and battered, slept in a chair beside her.

Camille was so thirsty. Dreams had swirled about her. Her head, her face, and her ribs ached. Nicholas. Meletios. Lavinia. Arabelle and Damaris. Genny and Kipp. One minute she was on the dance floor in Nicholas' arms and another Meletios stood over her with a knife. Penley's horrid face loomed before her, his cruel mouth laughing at her. Her whole body throbbed with pain.

"How'd you get those ropes off and where'd you learn to throw a knife like that?" Nicholas smiled through a swollen and cut upper lip. His right eye was nearly swollen shut. He'd woken up, leaned closer to inspect her face.

"I'd been working to loosen the ropes. Slipped my wrist through it as you were fighting. As for knife-throwing, I learned it by playing tavern games. Came in handy. Where'd *you* learn to fight like that?"

"Would you believe defending myself from my older brother?"

"I would, having met the odious man."

Nicholas laughed and then grimaced. Camille reached out and traced a finger over his lips. "You're hurt...."

He flinched and she drew her hand back. Heat rose in her cheeks.

"Just some bumps and bruises, bruised ribs, swollen knuckles, and a dislocated thumb."

She frowned. "If you hadn't come...if you hadn't found me ...."

"Don't think about that right now. You're safe. You're ..." he looked into her eyes, "home."

Camille chewed her lower lip and didn't meet his eyes. "Is Meletios ..."

"Dead? Yes."

She closed her eyes. "I killed a man ..."

330

He took her hand gently in his. "Meletios beat you viciously and was going to kill you," Nicholas said, his eyes like hard, glinting gold. "He certainly wanted to kill me. Henree too. I wanted to punish him…I should've shot him …."

Camille's eyes locked with his in alarm.

Nicholas turned serious. "The man killed men and women alike, took glee in torturing, beating, and maiming them. You will not feel one ounce of guilt, Camille."

"If only it were that easy, Nicholas. But you can't tell me what to feel. Or," she lowered her eyes, "what not to feel."

She looked up at him shyly. His eyes continued to burn into hers, seeming to reach into her womb.

"Do you feel something … for me?" he asked.

There was a knock on the door before Camille could answer. Genny waltzed in followed by Kipp, Josephine, and Henree.

"She's awake!" Genny said. Nicholas stood and stretched. "Don't stay long," he said, "she needs her rest." He looked into her eyes and left.

There was much chatter and fuss over Camille. She was thanking Henree for saving her life when she started to drift to sleep. Henree was looking at Josephine; there was no mistaking the intensity in his eyes. It made Camille smile.

"Hard men only loiter on the edge of boxing," Henree said. "Boxing takes skill. Huge gulf between a man trained in the ring and a street thug like Meletios. Never mind his size."

By now Camille recognized her grandmother's subtle expressions. Josephine looked like she was trying admirably not to roll her eyes at Henree while shooing everyone from the room.

57

The breeze from the bayou fluttered the curtains and made

the candles flicker softly beneath their glass cylinders. The moon

outside Camille's window was full, pale moonlight floating along

the water in silver tongues. Camille could hear the faint trickle of a

fountain from the gardens below and mockingbirds as they sang their

fluid melodies.

Magnolias, roses, and jasmine spilled their fragrances on the

night air. She was in the bedroom adjoining Nicholas' room, no

longer in his bed. Had she ever been? Or only dreamed it?

She wasn't sure how much time had passed since Nicholas

and Henree had managed to find her and bring her back from

Meletios horrible hideout. Days? Weeks?

She hadn't seen Nicholas much since he'd brought

her…*home*. She'd started to think of it as home. Perhaps she

shouldn't.

Had he really said, "You're home?" Or had she only dreamed

that as well?

She lay in the four-poster mahogany bed. A vase of fresh flowers sat next to the majolica pitcher on the washstand. Had Nicholas brought them?

Her body, her bruises, were nearly healed now. But her stomach clenched at a new thought. Maybe Nicholas was avoiding her because now that she was healed…there was really no reason for her to stay, was there?

Then why had he come for her in the first place? Because she'd saved his life once? Did he merely feel guilty? She was confused and whenever she thought about him, which was all the time now, her heart ached. She stood, crossed to the window, gently pushed the curtain aside. The breeze felt cool on her face. She was perspiring lightly beneath her nightgown.

She frowned, thinking that soon enough it'd be winter, with its hunting parties and suppers and family visits and trips to town, Christmas and New Year's. And where would she be? At Josephine's? Christmas at the plantation must be wonderful. She could imagine the great house, its white columns blue in the moonlight, the merry dancers inside, twirling and laughing. Ivy hung in wreaths on the white columns, soft lamplight streaming through an open door and firelight flickering on the window panes. How good it would be to feel she'd finally come home to a familiar place. Stockings passed out, laughter, the delight of Arabelle and Damaris when they opened their gifts.

Camille wiped a tear from her cheek, thinking it wouldn't do to have such fantasies. Would Lavinia be installed here as Nicholas' mistress?

She bunched her fists in the folds of her nightdress. Lavinia didn't care about the girls. She didn't care about Nicholas. From far off came the chattering of a screech owl. Camille paced, thinking of Nicholas' dark hair, the laugh lines around his hazel eyes and his mouth. She wanted to trace those lines leisurely with her fingers. She grew warm between her legs and her nipples hardened against the fabric of her nightgown.

She was like a woman in a dream. She held her hand up in the pale moonlight, the simple ring he'd given her still on her finger. Surprisingly, Meletios hadn't stolen it.

She didn't want to be a woman in a dream. She wanted to be *real*. She wanted to matter to Nicholas. Feel his hot breath on her neck, her lips, hear his whispered words and sensual groans in her ear.

She curled up in a chair by the window to wait, listening for the sound of his strident footfalls on the polished wood floors. She decided she was going to fight. She'd never purposely seduced a man before. The thought both frightened and intoxicated her. Could Nicholas ever think of her as more than a tavern waif? As someone who'd been forced on him by the selfish motives of others?

58

"You want to *what*?" Nick said.

"You heard me," Kipp replied.

Nick was speechless and that didn't happen often.

He poured himself and Kipp glasses of cherry brandy,

handed Kipp one, and sat down behind the massive oak desk in his

study.

He raked a hand through his dark hair. A hundred images of

Genny and himself as children ran through his mind. Scouring the

swamps for wild grapes, riding their ponies through the brush,

laughing and swimming in the river. They'd even, once or twice,

smoked corn-silk cigarettes behind the stables.

"She's not like other women," Nick said. "She's special and

…."

"I know. That's why I love her."

Nick almost spit his brandy out.

"Why so surprised I'm in love, chap? She's a beautiful, kind, engaging woman. And I want to make her my wife more than anything in the world."

"And you want my permission to ask her to marry you."

Kipp's sandy eyebrows danced. "Cheerio, lad. I'd *prefer* to have your permission but …."

"You're going to ask her anyway."

"Straight away, mate. Before someone else does."

Nick shook his head and smiled. "Well then, permission granted. But you'd better be good to her."

"No doubt about that, chap. For the rest of my life it will be my mission," Kipp beamed.

Nick stood and walked around the desk. "I'd be honored to have you as a brother-in-law." He embraced his good friend and gave him a slap on the back. They raised their glasses, clinked them together.

"What if she says no?" Nick mused. "She's turned away every suitor that's asked so far."

"I'm not every suitor, now am I? I think she actually likes *me*." He winked and left soon after.

Nick sat down again, drained his glass. His heart ached in happiness for Kipp and Genny. He stared out a tall window aware of another tender ache in his heart. Fireflies shimmered and blinked in the topmost branches of the trees. The stars were so bright they almost seemed blue.

He thought of the blonde-haired waif upstairs. He'd been avoiding her, afraid to go to her. He wasn't sure why. Maybe because he'd behaved so horribly to her.

He felt himself go hard beneath his breeches as he thought of her soft skin, sensuous lips, the way her eyes revealed all of her emotions. No woman he'd ever been with had looked at him like that. Plenty of women desired him, yes. But this was desire and something else. Everything she felt, whether she knew it or not, was naked in her eyes. *He was afraid of how much he wanted her.*

He groaned softly in frustration as he recalled what if felt like to part her slender thighs, to be between them, inside her, thrusting deeply until there was nothing separating them, her soft lips

339

whispering his name, the world disappearing with each heated breath.

He was painfully aware of how stiff and full his erection was.

If only he could show her what it could be like between them. So different from that first time in the rose-covered gazebo. When he'd come too quickly. When he'd realized too late she'd been a virgin.

But it was too soon. With all she'd been through ….

He startled himself with the realization that *he wanted her to come to him.*

59

Josephine came awake to the sound of strange scratching noises outside her window. "Oh stuff and bother."

She gathered her robe about her pajamas, white silk with blue satin stripes, and ventured outside to the small, second-floor balcony.

Dome-like trees shrouded in trailing green-silver moss spanned out thickly; the river beyond murmured sleepily. It was a cool, pleasant evening.

She'd been staying at the Branton plantation since they'd rescued Camille, brought her back from that odious man. Josephine was glad Nicholas had invited her to stay. She would've refused to leave her granddaughter at any rate. She was a stubborn woman and knew it.

She started as Henree landed with a thud next to her. He'd actually climbed a trellis from his room below and crawled over the railings to her balcony. That would explain the scratching sounds.

It caused her no small amount of consternation that he'd been invited to stay on as a guest too, and in the room below hers. She hadn't been sleeping well at all.

"Are you crazy, Henree? You could've used the door."

He wore men's pajamas, red. They were kind of silly looking at that. Still, Josephine tried hard not to think about the firmly muscled arms, chest and legs beneath them.

"Crazy only for you, Madame. And this was more fun than using the door."

Josephine sucked in a breath and felt tears brim.

She looked out across the rolling gardens. A breeze ruffled her thick silver-gray hair, which hung in a single braid over her shoulder.

"Henree, you helped to save my granddaughter's life," she said quietly. "For that I will always be grateful. She's all I have left. But …."

"But what Josephine?"

"But … you *left* me when I needed you most." She clenched her fists at her side, not knowing what to do with them.

He stepped closer, raised his fingers to her hair, caressed the braid, then pressed his lips to her neck.

"Mmmmm," she groaned softly before jerking herself away.

Henree grunted in frustration. "Josephine, you are the most obstinate woman!"

She liked the sound of her name on his lips. Most of their lives their relationship had been so…formal.

"I left you because I wanted to come back to you as a *man*. Not as your butler. Not as your goddamn servant."

"Henree!" Josephine looked into his blue eyes. "I don't understand Henree … you …."

He lifted his hand to her cheek and softly caressed it with his rough knuckles.

"To love someone from afar … why didn't you go to her then? Why did you stay with boring old me all those years?" Josephine whispered.

"Woman, I know you aren't a dolt but you *aren't* listening to me!" He grabbed her and easily hoisted her over his shoulder. Josephine beat her fists against his wide back but it was a feeble protest.

"*You're* the woman I've been in love with all these years Josephine! Only you."

She laughed and her heart filled with an incredible joy. He carried her to her bed and set her down gently. "I've waited a long time for you and I'm not sleeping alone tonight," he growled.

"Oh Henree," she sighed. "I'm an old woman now."

"You're a beautiful, desirable woman," he said, his lips sliding down her neck….

60

Camille murmured softly into a sturdy chest. Strong arms lifted her from the chair she'd fallen asleep in. "Nicholas?" she said sleepily.

She felt herself being lowered into her bed. "No," she said. Camille felt his body tense.

"Take me to your bed," she said.

"Are you certain?" he asked, his voice gruff.

Her arms went around his neck. She inhaled his masculine scent. "Yes."

"You've been through so much Camille. I don't want you to think you have to come to my bed because I saved your life. I don't want you to regret it...."

"You don't want me?" she said quietly.

"Oh I want you," he said, the evidence of his arousal pressing against her. "But ..."

"Then kiss me."

He slid her down his body slowly, yet not releasing her, so they stood toe to toe. His arms circled her waist. Her hands skimmed the fabric of his shirt, seeking the heat beneath.

Her words had made his heart thunder. "I want you to be sure Camille."

In answer, she went on tiptoe, her fingers curling behind his neck and raking his dark hair. Tentatively her lips brushed his. He pressed her closer. A sound broke from his throat and his mouth took hers hungrily. He swept her into his arms and took her to his bed, where he set her down gently.

Still leaning over her, their lips tasted each other, searching at first tentatively and then more eagerly.

He stood and Camille watched him unfasten the buttons on his shirt and tug it free of his trousers. He flung it off and the trousers and black boots followed. She stared at the muscles in his arms and chest, the soft thatch of dark hair below his navel, the taut, sleek lines of his thighs. She gasped at what was between them, his aroused manhood.

In the light of the fire from the hearth, Nicholas looked magnificent. His hair was black as night; his eyes tawny gold and intense as she'd ever seen them.

His skin was so smooth she ached to touch every inch of it.

"Come here," he said.

She obeyed.

He kissed her neck then took her mouth again, fiercely, commanding. He stood back from her then walked to the bed and lay down in it. "Undress for me, in front of the fire."

She turned her back to him and shyly lifted the voluminous nightdress over her head, discarding it on the floor. Her chemise and small satin undergarments followed. She turned and the look in his eyes, as if he would devour her, was startling.

347

His eyes roved over her legs, the gentle swell of her hips, her breasts. Then met her face.

She chewed her lower lip.

"What are you thinking?" he said.

"The look in your eyes … I'm not sure if you hate me or… desire me."

A rumble of masculine laughter was her answer. Then Nicholas turned serious, his eyes nearly burning through her. "I desire you…as I've desired no other woman. And I will prove it tonight."

His chin hardened. His eyes narrowed, taking in her loveliness again. His face was a fighter's face. One that welcomed, even reveled in battle. But she'd learned it could also be the controlled face of someone who'd learned early not to reveal by his expression his inner thoughts or feelings.

She couldn't help it; he'd always affected her. She could feel his presence the minute he walked into a room.

"Come here," he said gruffly.

She stood by the bed, her eyes lingering on his face, his chest.

"What do you want, love?" he said gently.

"I want to touch you," she whispered. "With my hands, my lips…. But I'm not sure I know how to please you."

He grabbed her, pulled her down so she was fully on top of him, pressed hot skin to skin, his arousal hard against her thigh. He kissed her deeply and her hands caressed his dark hair, traced the laugh lines around his sensuous mouth.

"Do what you wish. I will guide you. We will learn each other," he said.

She sat up and her hands found their way to his chest. She touched, caressed, was mesmerized by his taut muscles, the sleekness, the dark hair. She circled his nipples with her fingers and he moaned. She lowered her lips to kiss and taste the same places where her fingers had lingered.

He watched her intently and Camille could feel his heart thumping, feel his pulse as if it were her own. Delicately, she traced the bruises on his face. Though they were fading, they were still visible. She touched his lips; a finger delved into his mouth and he sucked it. A moan escaped his lips and he ground his hips into her side.

She did not rush.

It nearly killed him but he was patient though his manhood throbbed and ached with need of her.

In the same deliberate, gentle process, she touched and tasted the taut skin of his stomach, the soft, dark swath of hair beneath his navel, then his thighs, his inner thighs. He trembled. "Christ Camille."

"Did I displease you?" she said.

"Quite the opposite. I don't know how long…."

She traced her fingers down his hair-roughened calves, even massaged his masculine feet. "Every part of you is so beautiful Nicholas," she breathed.

His hands reached for and cupped her breasts and she gasped at the heat in his fingers.

His breath came faster as he tweaked her nipples, causing a deep wetness between her legs. He drew her between his open legs.

"I want to…taste you, all of you," she said, grasping his manhood in her fingers. The heat branded her. He threw back his head and moaned, guiding her mouth to his manhood.

"Take me in your mouth before I explode," he commanded.

Her fingertips tested the hardness of his muscles before her soft, pink tongue licked his shaft, then the tip.

He jerked. "Ah, yes, that's good, very good," he said.

Each kiss she gave was both a gift and a torment. And then she took him in her mouth.

His hands tangled in her hair as his head moved back and forth across the pillow. Camille found herself trying to memorize him with her lips-his shape, his color, his smell, the pulsing hardness of his manhood as Nicholas arched his neck in pleasure.

He groaned. "I'm going to come. I don't want to yet."

Nicholas rolled her beneath him and parted her thighs with his hand. His fingers delved between her legs and she cried out, sharp and sweet. Her hands fluttered over his back and she spread her legs wider.

"That's it love," he whispered. "You're more than ready for me, aren't you? This time it will be much more pleasurable for you."

Camille couldn't speak. Instead her lips found his and her tongue delved inside, pulling and teasing. He let her explore his mouth as he pushed his fingers into her with deeper, stronger thrusts. When he could stand it no longer, he kissed her savagely until her lips were swollen with his kisses.

Overwhelmed with pleasure, he rammed himself inside her. His hips swelled and rolled with his thrusts; she cried out in pleasure.

She wanted their lovemaking to heal them both, to wash away the bruises, the hurts, the misunderstandings. The things they'd been and hadn't been to each other, find what they could be to each other.

His dark head lowered; he suckled her breast and heat spiraled between her legs, shot up her spine as she clenched around him.

She gripped his shoulders, pressing him further into her.

He drove harder now and the ache built between her legs.

"Nicholas?" she breathed.

"It's ok, love. Let me take you there..."

He seemed bigger than ever inside her, hot and hard, pushing to her very core. And then he withdrew.

Her eyes were half slits of pleasure. "Nicholas?" she mewed.

"Turn over, on your knees. I like it this way. I think you will too."

She did as he asked, helpless, submissive, aching to be filled again.

He was on his knees behind her, his hands gripping her hips. He thrust inside her, hard.

"Oh God Nicholas, that feels...Oh God..." Camille said.

His hips moved in and out and she matched him movement for movement.

"Jesus, Camille. You're so beautiful."

Stabbing white hot waves rolled over her until her body stiffened and arched. She called out his name and was lost in a feeling so intense she found herself crying. His body stiffened and shuddered and he released a wash of hot seed in her womb.

When their hearts thundered back to normal he lay beside her and wrapped her in his arms.

"It's not always like that between two people, is it? I mean, so beautiful, so hard and soft at the same time, I felt like I was part of you," Camille said.

He smiled, traced a finger down her cheek, over her soft lips. "No, it's not always like that."

They lay there a while and her nipples grew hard as he caressed her. He kissed her and stirred another round of heat between them.

They made love two more times that night before they fell asleep.

61

The next few months passed quickly for Camille. It was

Christmas Eve. Guests were arriving at the Branton plantation.

Horses stood with lowered heads near the stable, pawing the earth,

waiting to be taken into the stable by the stable boys. The animals'

warm breath was visible in the frosty air, their rough coats caked

with splashed mud.

"Merry Christmas!" came out of the darkness often as old

friends greeted each other gaily. The house was festive and alive

with decorations, the smells of tantalizing food, and merry making.

Candles flickered in the great ballroom where the guests danced.

Camille had taken Passion for an invigorating ride earlier in the day, and when she'd finished, the huge house had been outlined for a moment against the sky, standing defiant upon the hilltop, its white columns blue in the moonlight, candles throwing a yellow gleam through the tall windows.

The house was filled with laughter; guests conversed and children ran and laughed, holding their red-and-white striped candy. Arabelle was her usual lively self; even Damaris had started to come out of her shell.

Mistletoe hung above doorways and Henree took advantage of it frequently to kiss his new bride Josephine. Pine boughs decorated stairways and mantels. Fires flickered in the fireplaces, throwing light on the high, dark ceilings and heavy beams and making reflections in the shiny goblets on the main tables. There was lively talk among the guests and the family; news of absent friends, messages passed on and repeated. Genevieve and Kipp were excited about their upcoming wedding, which would take place on New Year's Eve.

This is where I belong, Camille thought. *I am finally home.*

Camille watched Nicholas with love in her eyes as he playfully ruffled Damaris' hair and joked with Arabelle. The girls raced off then in search of some other sweet and he turned, as if he felt her watching him. He strode toward her, sweeping her into a shadowed alcove. "My love," he whispered. "You look so serious. Are you not enjoying the festivities?"

"I love you so much, Nicholas," she said, tears of happiness brimming in her eyes. "Our 'official' wedding a few months ago, all of this, the look of love in your eyes, it's like a dream. I never thought anyone could love me the way you do."

He kissed her fiercely. "Never doubt it my love, never."

He searched her eyes and pulled her closer. "I love you Camille. God, I love you. I thought…a forced marriage would be like my father's. I fought my feelings for you at every turn. Until I couldn't anymore. What a fool I was for wasting time! And how wrong I was about what it would be like to be your lawfully wedded husband. You came to me a grubby urchin' and transformed into the most beautiful, stubborn, sweet, seductive and beguiling woman I've ever known."

"Nicholas," she breathed, guiding his hand to her stomach. "Soon we'll have an urchin' of our own…."

His dark eyes grew wide and searching. "Is it true? You are with child?"

Camille nodded. He wrapped her tightly in his arms and then stepped back to behold her. There were happy tears in his eyes. "Come with me, let me show you something."

She took his hand as he led her outside to the great front porch and around the side gallery where it was dark and quiet. There was enough light coming through the windows to show her what he wanted her to see.

He pointed to one of the tall white columns. "See these carvings? Genevieve and I carved our names and these marks when we were children and measured ourselves against them. Arabelle and Damaris made their marks too. And now our children will do the same." Camille traced the carvings in wonder with her fingertips.

Music from the ballroom inside floated on the night air. Nicholas grasped her by the waist. "You're home, Camille…with me, where you belong…."

THE END

www.ingramcontent.com/pod-product-compliance
Lightning Source LLC
Chambersburg PA
CBHW020822180626
46814CB00001B/67